Saving Lucky

Isabella Alvarez

ISBN-13: 978-1469965420

Printed in the United States of America

February 2012

For everyone, and anyone, who inspire me ... you know who you are!

Prologue

Sometimes, things don't happen the way you want them to. Oh, you're having a great time, and you'd like to stay for a while longer, or you'd like someone else to stay for a while longer, and then - poof! They, or you, disappear.

That's what happened to me, Abigail Forester, when I traveled all the way from Russia to Antarctica, on a small plane with my parents, a suitcase, and some reluctance to leave my friends back in Moscow behind.

There was a special, a *very* special, animal that came into my life, once I got to my destination. She was absolutely incredible, magical, impressive, amazing, cute, cuddly, wonderful... almost anything I could ever imagine wouldn't be enough to describe her. She was... well, she was simply herself. She was who she was.

I grew very attached to this animal, spending a whole lot of time with her, laughing and singing and thinking of everything we might do, maybe if someday she could ever come out of her aquarium.

I never really thought about losing her, leaving her, or saying goodbye. I suppose that was good, not to concentrate on the sad things, just to concentrate on the positive, but it didn't help me in the end. I couldn't face it at first, leaving her? How could I?

Then something dawned on me, something came to me, and I knew, at one point everything has to go from one place, and move on to another, whether it was a person moving from one country to another country, or a person moving from life into death. Everything would have to go.

And when finally, when I finally had to let her leave, something struck inside of me, something made me let go. I realized that what I was feeling was the right thing, and I just needed to understand.

I guess that's what mattered in the long run, that I had to let her go, even if I hadn't wanted to, because she meant so much to me. I wanted to save her. Saving Lucky.

Chapter One

I stared out the window of the bouncing truck. A few snowflakes slid down the smooth glass, making me gasp in surprise as their intricate patterns weaved in a beautiful, dancing picture. It reminded me of the way my life was so hectic, so deranged.

My parents were always on the move. They *were* traveling scientists, after all. Mom was interested in animals, mostly; I got my creature-loving trait from her. My dad, he liked the climate more. He studied global warming, and increasing temperatures.

Naturally, we'd been all over the place. Zambia, Africa had been my favorite from what we'd seen, with the gorgeous, majestic cats sprawled out on rocks, and elegant giraffes bounding at a surprising speed. Colombia, South America was my close favorite. I loved how there were oceans, mountains, snow, and deserts all wrapped in one country. The food was amazing as well!

And now, I was in a truck, on the way to a research station in Antarctica, chugging along at an unreasonably uncomfortable speed. My mother sat next to me, her eyes wide as she took in our scenery. Of course, knowing her, she was actually searching for any kind of animal. My dad was the one who was looking at the surroundings.

I had to admit everything was pretty. The snow seemed to

be perfectly aligned in small clumps, the flurry was coming down in good amounts; the ice was gorgeous, frozen in masses all over the ground.

"Scientists, here we are at the McMurdo Station!" the driver's voice crackled over the speakers. My eyes matched the size of my mom's as I took in our new surroundings.

A gigantic bulldozer rolled down a path, scraping snow out of the way. A group of about six people bundled in thick, furry parkas ran in front of our truck. A couple of scientists yanked a metal cage into a nearby building.

"Wow," I breathed. My mom smiled knowingly, like she was saying, *of course, I knew you'd love it. See? Our fight was worth it all*. Oh yes, the fight. I'd had quite a few of those before. It was simply to prove my point that now, I was entering the age of teen-hood, as I liked to call it, and I did not want to keep moving around every three months.

The voice on the speakers tore me from my distractions. "Thanks to all of you scientists, now the United States of America can learn more and more about the ever-changing Antarctica! It was a great decision on your behalf to join us here, at the lovely McMurdo Station. Now, we're going to transfer onto Ivan the Terra Bus!"

I jolted at the unusual name. Since my parents were also in love with ancient history, I knew all about Ivan the Terrible. But this, a bus? Named after him? I watched in amazement as a huge red vehicle pulled up behind us. The tires smoothly slid in the snow,

4

stopping carefully when it reached our miniscule-by-comparison truck.

Ivan's big red, gleaming doors swooshed open. I grinned over at my dad, whose jaw was gaping open in a huge 'O'. "Never seen anything like it," I heard him mutter under his breath. It *was* impressive. I couldn't wait to file inside the enormous bus and get cozy in one of the seats. The truck didn't have a good heating system though, so I was forced to snuggle in two thick parkas.

"Come on, keep it moving!" the truck driver yelled as he rallied us out the door. "Have a great stay!" I plunked a five-dollar bill in his gloved hand before flouncing away. It worked every single time. He followed me, thanked me, and helped me onto the bus like I was a princess, all the while still muttering his utmost sincere thanks.

I stepped into Ivan, and away we went. The thing chugged along at a good speed, surprisingly, although I guess my criticism wasn't valuable because the only McMurdo vehicle I had ridden in before this was a bruised truck. Ivan rumbled over a couple big hills of snow, and finally, we were going down a main road. On each side of us, there were buildings everywhere- most of them simple structures clearly intended for work, not comfort.

Our ride with Ivan was much shorter then the one before. It was only about a ten-minute drive, and I had enjoyed myself on the Terra Bus. "I wish we had these when we were back in Russia," my mom murmured softly. "Oh, Johnny would have had such a fantastic party if he saw one of these! He would go on and on about the carpooling thing! Yes! And how it would eventually stop the

5

global warming effect. Of course, I'm brilliant."

I laughed to myself and hurried after the group. We all huddled in one big clump, which almost reminded me of penguins. I couldn't *wait* to see those creatures. In fact, that had been part of Mom's argument! "But you love birds, right?" she had said. "And penguins are birds! Don't you see, Abbie? Antarctica is perfect for us."

After a couple minutes, we arrived at a rather large building. There were beautiful ice crystals hanging down from the top, arranged in a disheveled, yet almost perfect way. Without hesitating, I pulled out my digital camera and snapped a picture of it. I checked the photo, disappointed that the electronic couldn't catch the true beauty of the glistening reflection, the geometrical symmetry that was etched into the sides.

"You'll have to make a scrapbook of everything you capture here," my dad told me, nodding. "I want to remember the McMurdo Station. It seems nice." Indeed, it did. I had researched their operating system, just the basics, one night on my computer. Everything was cool here, literally as well. No wifi?

The temperature went up about sixty degrees once we got in the building. It was eighteen degrees Fahrenheit outside, so in the building it was a toasty seventy-eight. I stripped out of my multiple layers until finally coming to a short-sleeved t-shirt and some khaki shorts I'd secretly put on earlier. My mom shot me a look, but said nothing.

"Hey, everybody!" someone, a girl probably, shouted to us

from behind. Our group whipped around and saw a lady smiling at us. She had on cozy sweatpants that read "McMurdo Rox!" and a short-sleeved t-shirt in the same style I had. "I see you're the new crew of scientists! Welcome. I know you'll love it here."

She motioned for us to follow her to the cappuccino machines. I quickly filled a cup with hot cocoa. I waited for it to cool down a little, and then took a sip. It was heavenly! "Please have a seat in the chairs we've arranged," the lady said. I sank down in the circle, still gulping my warm drink.

"I'm Amanda Tessler, the main gal here at Climate and Geography Studies," she went on to explain. Amanda walked around the circle, smiling at all of us. I could see why the chairs were arranged that way. "However, my studies aren't the only subject we provide scientists with here. There are Animal Studies, Glacier and Ice Studies, Human Infractions Studies..." Amanda listed out a whole bunch of other topics without taking a breath.

I waited patiently until she finished. "Is there anything for kids to do?" I asked, when Amanda was done. "I mean, sorry, hi, I'm Abbie. My parents are scientists- and I was just wondering whether I could do something scientific-based here."

She had a funny expression on her face, and I realized with reluctance that she was going to treat me like a little child. *Amanda: on the dark side*, I thought, making a mental note. I always came up with a list, everywhere I went with my parents. There was the dark side, and there was the light side. All the people I ever met would go on that list. It reminded me of being like my mom, classifying different species.

"Darling, of course! You could tag along with your parents, or perhaps another scientist who's free to have such a gorgeous child come along," Amanda practically cooed. I gritted my teeth. "But I'm afraid there are no true scientific activities you can participate in. You know what I mean by all that, right?" She got a fake-worried expression on her make-up smothered face. "My vocabulary might-"

"I'm thirteen," I growled. "And I am on a high-school writing program." My eyes were barely slits as I stared at Amanda, who simply laughed a stressed chuckle. She continued to blab on and on. I silently finished my hot cocoa, droning out the meaningless words.

So much for my dreams of becoming a scientist and following in the footsteps of my parents. I thought that the research stations like this one were supposed to cultivate young people's interests in Antarctica! *Wow, Amanda, way to be a true scientist.* I contained my need to loudly snort.

"Alright folks, looks like we're done here!" Amanda squealed finally. I rolled my eyes and kept examining the poster on the wall that I had been looking at for the past hour. "Are there any questions?" That caught my interest. I watched, surprised, as my mother raised her hand.

"I was wondering - *do* you have any programs my daughter could enroll in?" she asked icily. *Go mom!* I cheered silently. I shared a sly grin with Dad. He was listening just as

8

intently as I was. "Really, Abbie is very smart, and I'd like to get her interested in the amazing history, and wildlife, here."

Amanda seemed taken aback. She straightened her shirt, which now I came to realize, looked much prettier on me. Amanda cleared her throat before responding. "Dr. Forester," she squeaked in a mouse's voice, "I assure you, if there was something for your dear girl to do, I would tell you that immediately."

"She's thirteen," my mom said simply.

After being practically thrown out the door by an all too eager Amanda, we hopped back in Ivan and made our journey to the housing units. I couldn't wait to just chill out. It had been a long flight, a long trip here, and an even longer 'welcoming' speech to sit through. I leaned against my mom's soft shoulder, yawning.

Ivan pulled up in front of an icy slope. I cocked my head to one side, confused. Did we have to climb this hill? I hoped not. I was way too tired.

Luckily, it was only Ivan's driver who got up from his seat. He told us to stay on the Terra Bus, and that he was just checking something out. The rest of us waited, and waited, and waited. We watched Ivan's operator disappear behind the slope. He stayed there for quite a while.

Suddenly, the driver raced back into our view. With a quick "no-time-to-explain-sorry", he ran to the back of Ivan, fumbled around in the trunk, grabbed some sort of net, and motioned for all of us to follow him. I ran after the driver as fast as I could in four layers. My thick, furry boots didn't do much good, either.

We arrived at the edge of sea-ice. I knew, from my dad *and* mom, that sea-ice was very dangerous. It could crack easily, and of course, I didn't want to drown. Ivan's driver cautiously put his foot on the opaque surface. The sea-ice did not crack. I breathed a sigh of relief and confidently padded after him.

"Here," he announced, pointed to a crack in the sea-ice. I gasped when I saw a little nose peeking out. It was some sort of animal - maybe a seal! I wanted to pick it up immediately, but knew I couldn't. For one, nobody who knows common safety rules would grab a live seal out of the water with their bare hands. And two, I had already made this clear: I didn't want to drown.

"What should we do?" Dr. Coulan asked from the back of our huddle. "I don't think Ivan was meant to carry animals." I could barely make out his words with his thick accent, although I got the main point. We would have to stay out here, and freeze to death, with this poor seal! We had to! We couldn't just give up like Dr. Coulan was suggesting.

Ivan's driver looked defeated. His shoulders slumped, he let the net fall out of his hands. "No!" I cried, just as the thick, knotted string covered the seal's hole. I knelt down and yanked the net from the seal's nose. With determination, I cracked the ice even more, so the seal could breath. My mom didn't even scold me, for the seal was so adorable.

It popped up just like that. If it were in a movie, there would have been a little baby noise to accompany the animated movement. The seal was pure white, with black specks all over its sleek skin. Her eyes were a deep, deep black; I could stare into their depths. I could tell the seal was innocent, a tiny, weak pup.

I had to help it. Even though everyone was committed to thinking that we were doomed, that we couldn't save this poor seal pup, even though they'd lost faith, I couldn't. More determination washed over me like a tidal wave. I grabbed the net from Ivan's driver's hands, and pushed it down into the icy water. The seal tried to struggle, but I didn't let up. After she was officially netted, I slowly brought it back up.

My mom didn't hesitate. She bent down to help me yank the seal onto the sea-ice, simply shaking her head and muttering something unintelligible. Later, I'd have to thank her for assisting me. "We *can* do this," I announced, turning my attention to our group. "We have to save her. Do you think that we're representing the McMurdo Station's name well if we just leave a helpless creature out here to die?"

Murmurs went through the crowd; they shook their heads like my mom had. Finally, someone spoke. The noise came from a small little lady at the back of our huddle. She was very short, and a bit chubby, only because of the thick parka that was wrapped around her entire being.

"No," she said, firm and loud. "Save seal. Be scientist." I knew, even from her broken English, that we were going to have one more supporter. Or maybe a couple more. The scientists eventually turned their shaking heads into nodding ones. They moved forward to lift up the seal and carry it back to Ivan.

Since there were about ten of us altogether, the seal made it back quite safely. I donated a spare jacket for the seal to lie on, while Ivan's driver got some loose cord so the seal couldn't move. I helped him wrap the rope around the pup's slippery skin, and scooted over to the seat next to her. I decided to call the seal Lucky, because it was lucky to be alive.

"It's alright," I whispered, when Lucky started making a yipping sound. I suspected it was due to missing her mom; I couldn't make any assumptions. Maybe Lucky was cold? Or hungry? I didn't think that Ivan carried emergency baby seal food, or some kind of heater Lucky could use, so I was on my own finding a cure for Lucky to stop whimpering.

Tentatively, I reached out to pet Lucky's skin. I'd always wondered what a seal felt like... would it be smooth or slippery? My fingers crept onto its head. *OH!* I thought. *It's so soft!* I couldn't think of anything besides the funny sensation. Lucky had a little bit of puppy fuzz all over her, making the cold water dry faster. It was an interesting adaptation, because I couldn't feel Lucky's hair when she had been pulled out of the freezing ocean.

"Mom?" I asked suddenly, making half of Ivan's passengers jump. I realized it had been very quiet in the Terra Bus. "Why does Lucky need fur? Doesn't she already have blubber inside?"

My mom looked up from staring at her lap. She smiled a weak smile. "Well, darling, since Weddell seals like Lucky, as you've named her, live in such a cold environment, they have a specially adapted fur coat, which has outer guard hairs that are almost impermeable to water. They also have a layer of underfur that insulates them. The underfur helps regulate the seal's temperature." I rolled my eyes at her scientific approach at the explanation, but had to thank her. Now I knew to cross off 'is cold' from the 'What Lucky Needs' list.

Ivan bounced along for a while, with me comforting my adopted seal child and the rest of the scientists talking amongst themselves. Dr. Coulan seemed very annoyed that we had ever agreed to take Lucky on board. He also got a temper when he learned Lucky's name.

"You treat the seal like a child!" he screeched. "Do not get attached to animals. You claim that we do not represent the McMurdo Station name well. Yes, you are 'right'! Treating seals like children! This *pup* may not even last our entire trip." An icy glare from the short lady made Dr. Coulan shut his mouth immediately.

Once we arrived at the housing units, Ivan's driver instructed us to wait while he got a crate to put Lucky in. We were going to carry Lucky to an emergency lab a couple yards away from the houses. I gulped when a scientist practically threw my precious seal into the box.

Ivan's driver knocked on the wooden door as soon as we reached the lab. "Yes?" someone called from inside. Ivan's driver mumbled something I couldn't hear, but it must've worked, because the door opened immediately. A man with wild, white hair was standing there, his mouth stretched out wide into a smile.

"Oh, Josh!" he cried, crushing Ivan's driver in a humongous hug. I smiled as I thought that he looked like a mad scientist. "What is it? Another gas leakage with that poor Terra Bus you're always lugging around?" The mad scientist laughed a crazy laugh.

Josh, apparently that was the name of Ivan's driver, shook his head and simply pointed to Lucky's prison. The mad scientist's eyes went wide. He ushered our assembled group into the lab quickly. The mad scientist introduced himself as Dr. Ophellen, and then rapidly dumped Lucky out of the box. He pulled out a couple of syringes and wet towels and set to work.

Dr. Ophellen carefully examined Lucky from every angle. He made note of four bloody scratches on Lucky's tummy that I hadn't seen. *I wonder where Lucky got those*, I pondered to myself. Soon enough, I was sure the mad scientist would tell us.

Dr. Ophellen then cleaned up the red ooze coming from the scratch marks and applied some ointment onto them. Surprisingly, Lucky didn't squirm or yip once. Dr. Ophellen wasn't so mad after all. He went straight on over to the light side!

After a while, we heard him gasp. It was a shock, really; he'd been quiet and unconcerned for the past few minutes while he'd been examining Lucky. "I know what happened to her," he said suddenly, a black, sinister shadow overcoming his pupils. "She was *captured*. By a *boat*."

A sudden slideshow of images played in my head. The first was of my mom, sitting down with me, explaining the bad news of how she'd tried to save some sort of local endangered fish, but a

14

fisherman had caught three of the last five, and all the others were female, so the fish would die out. The second image was a vivid play of Lucky's capture: a net strangling her, making it unable to breath... her flopping around on the boat... the fishermen sighing and throwing her back into the ocean. And finally, I saw myself, crying, as I shoved a cremated Lucky under a deep pile of snow.

"Then catch them!" I yelled. "Catch those stupid people!" Sure enough, the tears came down in a flash. I couldn't control myself. Who would hurt such an innocent creature like Lucky? Wasn't she just the most adorable little Weddell seal ever? My mom wrapped her arms comfortingly around my shaking figure.

"Shhhh, Abbie," she whispered in my ear. "Lucky will be fine. Everything is okay. Lucky's safe, all right? That's the most important detail we cannot forget." I nodded; it was true. She had survived the evil, cruel, heartless people who'd dumped her back into the ocean. Another picture came to my mind, but this time, it was a happy one. I saw me and Lucky lying on the snow together, me in about five parkas, Lucky simply with her extra underfur and all those things Mom told me about.

"I'm sorry," Dr. Coulan said, all of a sudden. He was standing upright, facing me with determination. "I was wrong. The seal is lucky indeed, lucky to have lived through all of this. We must catch those evil-doers, and set their hands in chains!" I caught his unusual enthusiasm, and everyone followed along in our laughter.

It was good laughter. It showed our support for Lucky, how we knew we had to stop people from doing this to other seals, just like her. Even my cute little seal pup felt our joy. She yipped her adorable yip, which only made us giggle louder.

"Lucky is lucky," Dr. Ophellen told us, as soon as we'd all calmed down. "But other seals like her aren't. Even if they do not get hurt in Lucky's certain way, Weddell seals need to constantly breath above water, so they scrape at the ice with their teeth. Eventually, their teeth wear down, and they starve to death because they can't eat." I looked over at Lucky glumly. I guess she was doomed for starvation as well.

"Can't we do anything to help Weddell seals?" I asked hopefully. Of course, Dr. Ophellen just shook his head. We all sat there, sad and defeated. Everybody wanted to help seals like Lucky, knowing how helpless her situation was! How she was so little, so carefree. I wished all seals could have a rescuer.

Reluctantly, Josh herded us up and got us back into Ivan. We thanked Dr. Ophellen profusely, for taking care of Lucky. He was going to keep her under careful watch for the next couple of days, and report back to us with all the details.

"I hope Lucky'll be okay," I murmured to my dad when Ivan chugged back along to the housing units. "Sure, Dr. Ophellen seems like a nice guy, but..." I broke off and simply sighed. Dad didn't say a word, just rocked me gently back and forth.

We were assigned to Building 9, which was the ninth building, of course. I tipped Josh on the way to our new dorm, not really expecting him to trail after me like a hotel valet. Of course, to my surprise, he did follow me, carried my bags, and thanked me just as profusely as I did to Dr. Ophellen. I didn't smile; I only said barely audible thanks, for it wasn't Josh who had made my day. No, Lucky had.

I climbed up the stairs, trudging up and up and up. It seemed endless. I realized how heavy my eyelids were, how my back ached. The whole experience had been fun, but exhausting. I heaved a sigh of relief when we reached our room, number 306.

"This is so cool!" my mom exclaimed, once we had opened the plain brown doors. I did have to agree, the dorm was incredible. It was bigger than most of the other dorms I'd seen in pictures, since there were three cots, two in one corner of the place, the smaller one, probably mine, in another. At one side, there was a simple bathroom with one sink and a shower.

In my corner, there was a small TV, which I'd read about while researching the McMurdo Station. They had three channels, one of them was a news reporting station from New Zealand. I would probably watch that everyday. I had a mini heater next to my cot as well. It was a good setup I had to admit.

"What time is it back in Russia?" I asked absentmindedly. "I'm tired." To accompany those words, I let out a gigantic yawn. My mom laughed and looked down at her pink watch. Her eyebrows popped up in surprise.

"Actually, around all of our bedtimes," she replied, her voice already sleepy. "It *has* been a long day, Abbie. Time to sleep." She walked into the bathroom, then my dad followed once she'd changed into her flannel pajamas. I eventually followed them. My legs felt sore as I tread across the carpet.

Once I was back, and cozy, in my bed, I turned on the television and flipped through the three channels. I stopped on the Australian Network; it surprised me how sunny Australia was compared to the cold of Antarctica. I grew tired again, and felt sleep come on my eyes.

Once I'd rested a while, though, I didn't feel the need to sleep at all. After checking on my parents, (to make sure their snoring wasn't phony, of course) I slipped on my bulky pants and jacket and quietly raced out the door. I dashed back down the stairs, careful to run lightly on my eager feet.

I shone my flashlight ahead of me, not stopping until I reached the lab. I knocked on the door loudly, but not too loud so as not to disturb the people back at the housing units. Dr. Ophellen opened it slowly, his eyes wide. "Abbie?" he asked, confused. "What – "

"SHH!" I whispered. "Just let me inside. I'll explain everything." With a reluctant sigh, Dr. Ophellen let me pass through the door and into the heated lab.

Everything was scientific and amazing at night. The fish tank had a light shining into it, almost looking glow-in-the-dark, the floor of the microscope was lit up bright green... almost all the gadgets were lit up. I giggled in amusement when I saw Lucky, swimming around excitedly in her mini-aquarium. Dr. Ophellen had it set up very well.

"This is incredible!" I told him as I twirled around, trying

18

to take in everything. "Lucky looks so happy right now." The doctor nodded proudly, then shook off his loftiness. He stared at me, eyeing me like I was an intruder.

"And what exactly brings you here, Abbie?" he said suspiciously. I sank down quickly in the chair he had pulled out for me to sit on. It was going to be a long story and a very long night telling Dr. Ophellen the whole thing. I had a fantastic idea - he needed to know it.

Clearing my throat, as if to do a scientific speech, I began. "Well, I was thinking about what you said earlier, about Weddell seals and their unfortunate position with that teeth loss you talked about. So, I thought, maybe if there was medicine that had some kind of teeth-strengthening vitamin in it, maybe we could give some to Lucky! And other seals like her!" From the crazed look on Dr. Ophellen's face, I knew it was not a scientific speech. At all.

"Hold on just a second," he muttered. Getting up with a surprisingly quick pace, the doctor ran to his computer. Dr. Ophellen clicked a few buttons then curled his fingers, asking me to come over.

I obeyed, and smiled when I saw the page. Maybe he'd found something that could help Lucky, for on the website, there was an article about making teeth stronger. I read it to myself, interested the whole way along.

Animals such as cows, sheep, goats, and horses all benefit from teeth-strengthening vitamins hidden in their daily foods. Some of those vitamins are regular calcium enhancers, such as Vitamin D.

But there is one thing that helps in great amounts: salt blocks.

Besides just incorporating the delicious taste of salt, there is a whole lot more to this simple treat for livestock. The mineral contents of this 'mineral lick' includes: calcium, magnesium, sulfur, phosphorus, potassium, and sodium, obviously. All of these contribute to healthy, strengthened teeth.

"Does the McMurdo Station have any salt blocks?" I asked immediately, hopping around on my furry boots. Dr. Ophellen laughed at my eagerness when he nodded. I couldn't believe it! Lucky and the rest of her seal friends might possibly be saved!

"However, you should know, this could be dangerous. If we are caught -" my heart soared when he said 'we are', did that mean Dr. Ophellen would do this with me? "We could get in trouble. It might be illegal to help animals like this, and not letting them abide to the true cycle of life."

"Yeah, but what about Lucky? We can't just let her go helpless." Those words changed everything. Dr. Ophellen looked over at her aquarium, where she was leaping around, as if laughing. Lucky was so innocent, so adorable - nobody could do anything to hurt her. I knew the doctor felt the same way I did about her.

"Once, I let an animal go helpless," Dr. Ophellen said suddenly. His eyes stared down at the tiled floor, gazing at the simple pattern. I cocked my head to one side, trying to show my sympathy. "It was a small penguin. Too small. The penguin had been born wrong, due to some kind of toxic chemical.

"Some other scientists and I were on a boat expedition, tracking a whale. Then one of our crew people pointed out a penguin, which was struggling in a crack. The sea-ice wouldn't budge. I got the boat to pull over, and I went over to help that penguin.

"It was flapping so *hard*, I couldn't believe the penguin was still holding on to its life. I tried to pull it out, but the sea-ice didn't crack. I tried that day - and I failed. Eventually, I had to keep going on my expedition, had to leave the penguin behind. When I came back, after tracking the whale, that penguin was gone. I knew it had drowned."

Had Dr. Ophellen really admitted all that to me? I didn't know what to do. I just squirmed around in my chair, uncomfortable. I looked over at Lucky, who hadn't noticed a thing. *At least she doesn't have to worry about awkward situations*, I thought.

"Well, you can make up for that one penguin," I announced to Dr. Ophellen. "By helping save another animal - a lot more animals." I could see the light coming into his eyes, making everything seem possible again.

I waited for him to realize my idea was a good idea, and the moment finally came. "Alright," he said finally, looking up from the floor. His face had changed. He was determined and ready to help save those seals. "When do we start?"

Chapter Two

I looked around, scanning the area for any sign of movement. Out of my furry pocket, I produced a crisp hundred-dollar bill and smiled. It was from Dr. Ophellen to buy three salt blocks, and have them delivered to his lab.

The supply building soon came into view. I hurried my pace up a couple notches, crunching across the mixture of volcanic rock and snow. It made a satisfactory sound that I had come to enjoy for the past week I'd been staying at the McMurdo Station.

I pushed the back door of the supply building open with a heave. A teenager in flannel pants and a thick hat looked up from a pad of paper. "What can I help you with?" he asked, grinning.

"Dr. Ophellen sent me to pick up some salt blocks," I said casually, folding my arms over my chest. I could tell the teenager wanted to play a 'cool' game. Well, I wanted him to know I could play, too. "I have some cash."

The teenager handed me a crooked smile and held out his gloved hand, where I promptly plopped my hundred-dollar bill. He licked his lips, considering something then shook his head. He disappeared in the sea of supplies and emerged a couple moments later, holding a small salt block. The teenager offered it to me; I frowned, puckering my lips in what I hoped was a grown-up way.

"No," I decided. I glared at him with a smirk. "Bigger."

After a couple minutes, I was in a toasty glass encased tractor, with a *huge* load behind me. Peter, the teenager, had hooked a crate, filled with my salt blocks, to the end of the bulky vehicle. We were listening to his CD. It had most of the bands I listened to, actually.

"I like this song," I said suddenly. Peter looked at me, and I blushed bright red. We were silent for the rest of our short-lived ride. I stared out the window, looking for the slope Ivan's driver had found Lucky behind. Peter sadly didn't drive past it.

Finally, the tractor rumbled up in front of Dr. Ophellen's lab, and Peter helped me unload everything onto the back porch. Once we'd transferred the salt chunks safely to where the doctor could find them, Peter said goodbye with a weird look in his eyes.

"No way," I whispered softly, watching the tractor pull away and disappear. "My little Weddell seal's secret could never be trusted with him." I sighed and knocked on Dr. Ophellen's door. I got to drag the slabs of salt near Lucky's aquarium while the doctor watched me.

I stood on a chair and cautiously put a salt block into the water. I stared at Lucky's every move as she nosed it around. She eventually began to look curious. *Yes, yes!* I cheered her mentally. Lucky stuck out her pale tongue and licked the block, at first hesitant and then a bit crazed. She licked like a maniac.

"I can't believe it!" I shouted. Dr. Ophellen laughed when I jumped around in a victory dance. "Our plan is *so* going to work," I said, once I'd calmed down a little. "If Lucky thinks the salt tastes good, then other seals like her will, too."

Dr. Ophellen couldn't say anything bad about that, so I just giggled and flounced out of the lab, shouting a carefree goodbye behind my shoulder. There was a full day ahead of me; I wanted to spend it perhaps with my mom, or dad, even. They were going on a tour of the McMurdo Sound.

My happy attitude was cut short when I saw the note on the door of our dorm room, once I'd reached Building 9. "'Dear Abbie - Mom and Dad are out on the tour we told you about. Be back around four p.m., Antarctica time. Love you,'" I read aloud, groaning. "Ugh. Now I have a whole seven hours with nothing to do."

I flopped down on my cot, which creaked under the strain of my weight. It was a small thing, the only thing besides me that would fit on it was my sweats. I decided it would be a good idea to change into those and my old school's sweatshirt. I turned the TV on, and watched the Navy channel for a while.

"Maybe a book would help," I mused out loud. I rummaged through my suitcase to find a battered copy of *Wuthering Heights*, so worn out that you couldn't see who wrote the book. Of course, I knew it was by Emily Bronte. I read for a couple hours, rotating from the television to the novel.

Finally, I couldn't take the strain anymore. With one smooth move, I hopped up out of the sheets, dressed back in my cold-weather clothes, and raced down the stairs onto the crunching snow. I ran with determination, pounding the soles of my boots into the ground. I raced all the way past Dr. Ophellen's lab, the dreadful place where Amanda resided, the 'mess hall', Ivan's gigantic garage, and finally, I reached the supply building. Peter was still there, whistling away.

"Hey," he said casually. "What's going on?" I felt my heart pound beneath the layers I'd put on. It was time. Time to tell him about Lucky.

"H-hi, Peter," I mumbled. "Um, I have something to show you." Peter raised his eyebrows in disbelief, like I wouldn't have anything to show him. However, he didn't object to being dragged out of the door to his tractor.

We drove to Dr. Ophellen's lab. I made him park four hundred feet away, so as not to disturb the doctor. He was probably absorbed in some kind of study, and I didn't want him to get distracted. The doctor, I'd found out, was absolutely brilliant. He definitely deserved that entire lab.

"Be quiet in there," I whispered to Peter. "We don't want to make Dr. Ophellen notice us much, okay?" Peter nodded and followed me in through the back door. He gasped in surprise at the amazing place, but I simply placed a finger to his lips.

"This is Lucky," I said quietly, pointing to my frisky pup's aquarium. The salt block had almost completely disappeared. "She was caught in a net, when a fisherman..." I explained Lucky's entire background to Peter in less than three minutes, which was nearly impossible for me to do. Well, impossible to do without Peter listening.

He cocked his head to one side when I finished. "Wow," he said finally. "That's why you needed those slabs." I nodded, letting him contemplate everything. "I could help you," Peter offered suddenly. He made his voice loud, so Dr. Ophellen could hear.

The doctor finally looked up from his microscope. "Hello, Abbie!" Dr. Ophellen exclaimed brightly. He turned to Peter. "And whom have you brought?"

Once introductions were done, I told the doctor that Peter wanted to help us preserve the Weddell seals. Dr. Ophellen listened to Peter's ingenious ideas for a long time. It seemed like Peter wasn't just a smirking teenager who worked at the supply building. He was truly a scientist at heart.

"Young man, I think that's splendid!" Dr. Ophellen's words were final. I felt like hugging Peter right then and there, but I didn't. I did a quick Abigail Forester Happy Dance to keep myself from swooping Peter up in a ginormous bear squeeze.

We talked for a while longer, and came up with some really great ideas to add to our Weddell seal repertoire. For one, we had to add some more vitamins to the salt blocks, since they came from the supply shack, which didn't have actual salt blocks that contained all the nutrients Lucky needed. Peter also thought of creative ways to help seals more safely.

"If more Weddell seals get these teeth-strengthening boosts, maybe when they have pups, the strong teeth will pass down from generation to generation," Peter suggested once. Dr. Ophellen and I both agreed that it was a fantastic hypothesis.

The doctor walked Peter to his tractor, said 'goodbye', told me he owed me a *huge* favor, and went back to his intense study under the microscope. I watched Lucky frolic around her aquarium for a couple minutes, and then walked to my dorm.

As soon as I was safely plopped down on the creaking cot, I whipped out a sketching pad and some charcoal pencils. I'd picked them up back in Russia, when drawing had been my passion. Now, I'd neglected my talent. I wanted to get it back.

I started off with a quick sketch of Lucky. I made her eyes anime-style, with bright bubbles in the middle, and color bouncing off the edges. Her tail curved over in a wave, almost. I liked it so much that I added movement marks so a viewer would see that she was saying 'hello' to them. I made Lucky's body curved and cute, hinting at the fact she was innocent and a young little pup.

On the next page I wrote a couple bullet points about Lucky's personality, her scientific information (courtesy to Dr. Ophellen; additional reference: Peter), and other things about Weddell seals. I put my time and effort into it all.

The final drawing in my trilogy was a bit like a warning poster, with the three main threats that Lucky's kind faced. I made the sketches gory; it was a bit unnecessary, but I wanted to show how sad it was that these innocent creatures were treated so cruelly.

I pulled out a mini-stapler from my mom's desk, and stapled my pages together. I taped a cover on the top of them, which stated what the packet was about. I would have to make a bunch of copies the next day. Maybe Peter would help me deliver them.

Just after I'd snuggled back down under the covers, my mom and dad burst through the door, still wearing their many layers. "Hey Abbie!" Mom exclaimed. She hung up her four jackets on the jacket hooks. "How was your day? Ours was fantastic. The guide, Dr. Smith, was absolutely brilliant. He was so - "

"Okay, okay!" I said, grinning. "That's great, guys. I think it's *dinner time*." I stretched out those words as if I was speaking to my students in a foreign language class. My mom laughed along with me, shrugging back into her parkas. Dad giggled sheepishly; he hadn't taken off any layers.

We crunched through the mixture of snow and volcanic rock, making a loud noise with our boots. Dr. Coulan, Dr. Reiso, Dr. Johnson, Dr. Brown, and other scientists I didn't recognize caught up with us on our way to the 'mess hall'. It almost reminded me of camp, going to the big dining hall, and helping ourselves to all the delicious food.

Nothing was fresh here at the remote McMurdo Station, because it took a long time to import freshly made or harvested food. I was just glad that we weren't forced to eat Spam. I hated processed food.

"They're serving lasagna today," Dr. Brown announced, as he sniffed the air. "You like that, don't you, Abbie?" She winked and laughed. Dr. Brown reminded me of a carefree little girl, spinning around in a field, not really caring about anything. She knew me well because of all the nights we'd spent at the s'mores fire every Wednesday. Tonight it was a story-telling bonfire, which I hadn't been to yet, but wanted desperately to go.

"'Course," I replied, smiling. "I wouldn't miss that lasagna for anything. Hey, are you coming to the fire at nine, tonight?" I directed my question to the entire group.

"Yes," Dr. Coulan told me. He was much friendlier to me now. We'd started off on a bad note; now, we were going to end on a good one. "The stories are fabulous, I've heard, tales of the greatest legends of Antarctica. Tales that make you shiver - even though the wood is burning hot, and you are sipping some delicious drink." We all laughed at his ever-present enthusiasm. Dr. Coulan had a way with words. If he weren't a scientist, he would probably write novels.

Dr. Johnson informed us that he did not feel good, so he would not be attending the fire. Of course, the other scientists nodded their heads to my question. The fires were fun for everyone. They brought us all together, and helped people make friends and science-mates.

"Get some food, then meet me at the fifth buffet area," my mom whispered into my ear, and pointed at a newly polished table. I nodded and grabbed a tray. I decided to work my way from the side dishes to the yummy main courses.

I grabbed a salad, a slice of bread, a heap of lasagna, and some apple cider. I would be having hot chocolate at the fire that night, so I didn't need an extremely sugary drink right now. On the way to the table, I snatched one of the famous butter cookies from a table. They were heavenly and I couldn't resist.

29

"Have you made any friends here?" my mom asked nonchalantly. I could tell where she was pushing at, and I definitely did not want to go there. It had been Mom's wish ever since I'd entered the whole teenage thing that I would get a true, caring boyfriend. Perhaps I'd have to ask Peter if we were together, but I decided against it. He was really just a kindred spirit who'd been incredibly nice to me.

"Well, I'm very good friends with Dr. Ophellen," I began, innocent as always. I could see my dad's (and mom's) expressions begin to slump. Perfect. "And then there's Dr. Brown, and Dr. Coulan. Since there aren't a lot other kids here, I don't have many friends."

The subject was changed, and I was happy again. I wanted to keep the secret that I even *knew* Peter. My parents would probably overreact. I didn't like my mom's squeals of delight, or my father's proud grin whenever I told them something like that.

"We have a while before the story-telling begins," my dad said after our meal was over. "Your mother and I are going to go star viewing, from the top of that big hill we passed on our way here. Stick to the main group, and meet us at the fire. Eight forty-five at the latest, okay?" I nodded.

When they had disappeared, I ran all the way to the supply building again. I wanted to have my own survival kit for the Antarctic. You never knew what could happen. A penguin could become vicious. A whale could knock me into the ocean! *Not probable*, I thought automatically.

30

"You again?" Peter teasingly asked, once I reached the back door and pushed it open. "What now, Abbie? Did you find an injured... squid?" I laughed at his wacky guess, simply shaking my head.

"I came to ask you for something," I informed him. "I just wanted to get some supplies together, like a survival kit, if you want to call it that. Okay, yes - it sounds weird, but I think my idea is genius."

Peter chuckled. "Yeah, Abbie, you're gonna get swallowed by an Antarctic shark, and your 'survival kit' will have an gun designed for Antarctic sharks." He laughed and got me some supplies, explaining how to use everything along the way. I ended up getting some pretty cool things.

We walked back to the fire, being careful not to show anything beyond the 'normal' signs of friendship. My mother and father would act like baboons. As I said before, I didn't want them knowing anything about my social life. Lucky was the only one who was truly 'lucky' to be able to get to know those kinds of secrets.

It was funny, really. I had grown so attached to her. I would not be able to let go of my adorable Weddell seal when it was time to do so. My stomach felt queasy again when I thought of that moment. I couple imagine her, slipping out of my grasp, back into that dangerous ocean...I would be devastated. Heartbroken. And not even Peter would be able to console me.

"Abigail!" I groaned inwardly when my mother called out to me, using my full name, and singing it in a girlie voice. "Who have you brought?" I knew Peter would know how to handle this, so I let him take charge. He simply shook my mom's hand, then told her his designation.

Peter and I took the two seats on a fluffy love seat. I wished those couches weren't called love seats - because my mom kept shooting me these really annoying looks. I could've just about curled up in a ball and never, ever woken up. I wanted to send her a telepathic message: *Peter is a FRIEND!*

"Hey everyone," a voice said. I looked over Peter's hat to see a slim, perky adolescent girl walking towards our group assembled around the crackling fire. "I'm Tina, and this is Mark." She motioned to a slightly older guy behind her. They both waved a cheerleader kind of swish.

Somebody passed around steaming mugs of creamy hot chocolate. I smiled in delight and took a huge gulp. It was the perfect McMurdo Station drink, just the way I liked it. Apparently, Peter enjoyed the cocoa too. He downed his cup in about two seconds flat as I watched giggling to myself.

"As you know, Antarctica has a lot of mystical legends," Mark said. He put his elbows on his knees, leaning forward in anticipation. I found myself trying to contain my excitement at this story-telling event. "Atlantis, for example, is one. But at the McMurdo Station, we've found some more *secret* tales."

Tina waggled her eyebrows and handed out a sheet of paper. On the top was titled, 'Legend of the Great Seal'. I smiled to myself, imagining Lucky with a crown placed upon her head and her commanding sea-creatures. I couldn't wait for their story to unfold so I began reading immediately, wanting to gulp down 'Lucky's' story.

There once was a young woman named Haki. She was swift as a fish, cunning as a whale, and smart as a snow rabbit. Her hair was long and black, always woven in a thick braid, so as to not disturb Haki when she was hunting. Her legs, thin and lanky, made Haki an incredible runner.

On a certain snowy day, Haki was walking on the ice. She made her steps light, hoping to keep the ice intact. Suddenly, she saw a curious thing: a hole in the ground! Haki crept her way over to the hole. She looked in and gasped in amazement.

I crunched my eyebrows after reading the short paragraph. I motioned to Mark and Tina that I'd read everything, not mentioning the fact I wanted to hear more of the story... where was the rest?

"Look!" Tina cried, pointing to something in the snow with an obvious theatrical element. She pretended to be amazed. "Come, look!" We followed her to the place she was pointing to. I gasped in astonishment. There, in a small, comfortable hole was a seal! It was absolutely adorable.

Mark ushered us quickly back to the fire, strictly forbidding us to look backwards. I snuck a glance, and saw that a team of scientists were rallying the seal back into the cage, and hurriedly whispering to Tina. I chuckled. They had made a great effort; they just needed to get the transporting of the creature down to a science.

"Haki, as you've guessed, saw a seal," Mark began. "Of course, the seal was there of pure coincidence, since she was out in nature. Here at the McMurdo Station, we simply brought out a healthy adult Weddell seal-" I grinned and made a mental note to alert Dr. Ophellen-"that one of our scientists found and is currently observing." I deleted the mental note altogether, for I knew it was the doctor who was studying this seal.

"*But*," Tina cut in, looking sharply over at her companion, "Haki's sight of the beautiful seal was not by coincidence, you see. That gorgeous creature was a messenger from the goddess of animals, Diana. Of course, in Antarctica, the goddess was known as Dian.

"Dian had seen Haki, hunting yet still treating animals kindly, showing her respect to the earth around her. She wanted to reward this woman with something great, something worthy of Haki. So Dian told the seal to ask Haki what she desired most.

"Haki replied to Dian's messenger, saying she wanted a thick coat, made of the utmost wonderful material Dian could find. Haki had been very cold in the winter months, and she could use more protection against the harsh gales of snow.

"The next morning, Haki found herself wearing a good coat, of course. Dian was a faithful goddess, so she had to fulfill all her promises. However, Haki was disgraced and cursed the goddess. 'How dare you!' she shouted to the heavens. 'You killed your own messenger just to make a coat!'

"Indeed, the seal's furry skin had been made into a coat for Haki. Dian had taken the life from that innocent messenger to grant Haki her wish. Haki was so distressed that she threw the coat into the ocean and threw herself in as well. Dian, seeing that Haki truly did feel sorry for the seal, decided to change the seal back into its living form.

"So then, Haki and Dian reigned in the skies forever, with the seal as their trusted messenger and faithful friend."

Everyone's eyes gleamed when Tina finished the tale. We were all imagining the story- it was so incredible. I loved how our storyteller had told it, with respect and suspense and drama. Tina acted everything out with exaggerated motions. Next to me, Peter was muttering something like, "Whoa. That was awesome."

"Well done!" a scientist shouted, and began to clap. Everyone joined in. Yes, it was well done. More than well done. Tina had done a fabulous job. I loved that tale - I loved imagining Lucky as the seal, myself as Haki, Dian as perhaps a female version of Dr. Ophellen, or maybe even Peter, although they'd never do anything so cruel.

On our way back to the dorms, my parents didn't pester me about Peter. They simply joined in my awed silence, contemplating along with me about the story we'd just heard. I couldn't wait for the next story-telling campfire. I'd have to check the schedule once we were at the main lobby of Building 9.

I trudged up the stairs, a little gloomy at the prospect of falling asleep. How could I sleep, with images of a be-crowned

Lucky and me, screaming at Dian for her darkness, floated around in my brain? I sighed as I pushed open the brown door to my dorm. I slipped into some fuzzy pajamas, hopped onto bed with reluctance and finally lulled myself to sleep.

The next morning I woke up to the sound of my mom's alarm clock. It sounded extremely annoying. I groaned and shoved the pillow tighter over my ears.

"Honey, *please* wake up," Mom grumbled, shaking me gently. "Time to wake up, sleepyhead. We're going to do some mother-daughter things today." That made me want to stay asleep forever, but I finally tossed the covers off my head.

After shoving on some of my favorite, fuzziest, coziest snow pants and the coolest parka I had, I ate a small breakfast of cereal and waited for my mom to discuss our 'mom-daughter' plans. I wasn't looking forward to this one single bit.

My plans had been simple: visit Lucky, sketch some more, chat with Dr. Ophellen, and maybe pay Amanda a little visit. I had some pretty intense dialogue in store for her. In fact, I'd practiced it last night before I had shut my eyes! *Great*, I thought. *Now I'm stuck doing Popsicle stick crafts instead of giving Amanda some of her own medicine.*

"I thought we could go see some Emperor Penguins!" my mom blurted out, once I'd slumped down to the lobby. She was bright and perky, with some binoculars hanging from her neck, and a folded brochure in one hand. My mom handed it to me to read.

"'Follow Dr. Smith on this expedition to the icy regions of

furry birds who can't fly.'" I sighed, not wanting to continue. My mom sent me a puppy look. "Isn't that the same guy who took you on the tour of the McMurdo Sound?"

Somehow, I was dragged onto a smaller version of Ivan, which I nicknamed Ivan Jr., and to an even shorter-nickname, Junior. Ivan's 'son' bounced along, crunching over the volcanic rock like a beast. Junior had only twenty seats, therefore boosting the quality of its ability to maneuver challenging terrain. It was painted a darker red than Ivan, probably so that people would be able to notice Junior if it ever got stuck in the huge mounds of snow.

"Now, we're passing the Discovery Hut," Dr. Smith practically shouted onto the speakers. *Why does my mom like his tours?!* I wondered. *All he does is yell.* With reluctance, I stared out the window and was amazed at what I saw.

The Discovery Hut was a small shelter made of grey wood, weathered from years of wind, snow, hail, and sleet. I couldn't wait to go inside, but Dr. Smith didn't stop the bus to let us out. Instead, he described it to us in a Dr. Coulan-esque way.

"There are several artifacts that Robert Falcon Scott brought here. In one corner, we have dusty boxes, filled to the brim with old, worn-out supplies. In another, there is a satchel that an early scientist might have used. The McMurdo Station honors all these artifacts very highly." I smiled and pictured 'early scientists'.

"We're going to get out here!" Dr. Smith called out. I got up from my cozy seat and followed my mom through the open doors. The wind slapped my cheeks so hard it made my eyes water.

The snow swirled around us in harsh flurries, much more harsh than back at our dorms, and Building 9, and the whole common-living area.

Dr. Smith led our small group to a flat area of snow. My grin turned huge as I took in the huddle of penguins. They were so majestic - yes, they were emperors. I watched a tiny chick squeak for its mom and chuckled. It reminded me a little bit of Lucky. Of course, penguins weren't like seals that much, in fact, seals *ate* them, but I still enjoyed watching the "furry birds that can't fly".

I got out my camera, the same one I used to take some pictures of Lucky, my cafeteria experience, the icicles, and now, the cute penguins. I checked the photo. It was absolutely gorgeous. I showed my mom, who loved it just as much as I did.

"That's great, sweetheart," she told me, nodding approvingly. "I love the way you got that family - see, there's the dad, the mom, and the baby!" I had never noticed that, but had to agree. My mom was fantastic at observing the behaviors of animals, so naturally only she could show me the fascinating family of birds that I hadn't been able to see. It was pretty amazing.

We spent an hour there admiring the penguins. Dr. Smith pointed out some characteristics about the birds, explaining lots of cool facts. I found out a lot of interesting details that I'd have to make note of in my sketchbook. I wanted to transfer my photo to my sketchbook as well.

"Sadly, it's about time to leave these grounds and go back to the station," Dr. Smith announced after our sixty minutes were up.

I was reluctant again, but this time I had to get back into my cozy seat and leave the penguins. They were absolutely adorable, although perhaps not as cute as Lucky.

The ride on our way back seemed much shorter than going *to* the meeting place. It really was no wonder why my mom and dad loved Dr. Smith's tours and expeditions. He explained everything so well he made you want to learn more, he made you fascinated, even if his shouting had to come with the deal. I couldn't wait to join him again for another journey.

When I got back to the dorms, I plopped down on the bed and bounced on it. The whole day had been so fun. To think, I'd thought I would've done Popsicle stick crafts! "Thanks for taking me, Mom," I called out diligently. My mother was taking a shower at that moment, so all I got was a muffled reply.

I didn't feel like sketching, or reading, or watching TV, really. I just kept bouncing on the bed, and thinking back to every bit of the tour. I finally decided on visiting Lucky. It didn't seem very fair to spend the day with penguins and ignore my Weddell seal.

"I'm going over to Dr. Ophellen's!" I yelled to my mom, and skipped out the door. The flakes outside were much more calm than the clumps of icy snow that poured over me when I was visiting the penguins.

The door to the lab was opened just a crack, so I tiptoed in, not wanting to disrupt the doctor's studies. He was always observing something when I came to the lab, and Dr. Ophellen needed time to work on his projects. Dr. Ophellen was a very dedicated man. I appreciated that.

"Hello?" I whispered into the air. It was crisp, and hung with an air of stale bitterness, as if nobody had been in there for a while. "Lucky?" At least she was still there. Lucky swam around excitedly in her aquarium when she saw me approaching. Just then, a hand clamped on my shoulder.

"I've been looking everywhere for him," Peter told me, once I turned around and was relieved to find it was him. His eyebrows were creased with worry for the doctor. I realized it wasn't just me who had a firm relationship with Dr. Ophellen.

"Where exactly did you search for the doctor?" I asked, raising one eyebrow like a suspicious detective. While he made us both some hot chocolate, from Dr. Ophellen's personal machine, of course, Peter told me his story. I drank from the plastic cup, the worry filling me up like my warm drink.

I wanted to call Dr. Ophellen, but that idea was ridiculous, because there was no cell phone reception and the doctor probably didn't have a phone, anyways. There really wasn't any way to connect to him, other than to talk directly.

"Ugh," I groaned.

"Ugh," Peter agreed. We sat there for a while, taking in the surroundings, thinking of how to find Dr. Ophellen. I couldn't possibly know where he would've gone, unless he had left on an expedition. Peter informed me he had even checked in with Amanda to see all records of the doctor's travels from the morning until this moment. Of course, Dr. Ophellen hadn't gone anywhere, at least not within the McMurdo Station... oh! An idea suddenly struck me.

"Hey, maybe he went out to find some Weddell seals," I blurted out. "The Station can't know about Saving Lucky. They think we've already released her, so then Dr. Ophellen couldn't have told them!" Peter nodded, contemplating my idea.

"You're onto something," he said finally. "But we can't go out to find him. It's getting dark already. In a couple minutes, we're going to have to go home." I nodded, holding back my disappointment. All I could do was wait for Dr. Ophellen to come back.

Chapter Three

I took a deep breath when I saw there wasn't anyone besides Peter in Dr. Ophellen's lab the next morning. I stripped out of my thick parka and kicked my boots up on the table, taking a sip of a decaf latte Peter had taken the time to make for me. It tasted nice; I'd gotten used to coffee back in Colombia, where the locals practically showered me with it.

"'Morning," I said, aiming the casual remark to Peter. I eyed his barely-touched latte and motioned to it. "Are you going to drink that?" When he shook his head, I grabbed the cup. With one steady gulp, I finished it all.

"How can you be so... so relaxed?" Peter asked me suddenly. His eyes were bloodshot, red from crying. He probably had bawled all night. "If I offered you a tray of delicious chocolate chip cookies, I bet you'd eat the whole tray, not even thinking once about the situation we're in."

"*Do* you have any cookies?" I joked. I was just trying to lighten the mood. Peter was so tense, so worried. He reminded me of a professor, or even a frustrated scientist. My dad had gotten like that once, when the weather reports crashed. He always needed to be informed about the weather, or at least what the climate would be like. After all, Dad studied climate change!

"Keep trying to be funny," Peter snapped. "You're hilarious." He made a fake 'ha-ha-ha' noise, which finally threw me into a fit of rage. How could he be like this? *Go back to England and be a sarcastic duke*, I thought, disgusted.

"Keep trying to be mean," I shot back at him. "You're absolutely nasty." We glared at each other for a few moments, trying at an unofficial staring contest. I, being the girl, won. Peter glared at me for a second more before sighing and straightening his jacket.

Suddenly, there came a knock from the door of the lab. Peter and I looked up, jolted from our fight. I raced to the door and yanked on the wooden handle with all my might. I grinned when I saw Dr. Ophellen standing there. However, his condition wasn't something to smile about. His normally well-kept hair was a complete disaster, flying in all different directions. His shirt was torn, the holes deep and sagging. His pants were fine, only because they were the standard snow-proof, everything-proof ones that the McMurdo Station required everyone to wear.

"Hello." Dr. Ophellen spoke in a ragged voice, making me jump. I heard a thud from the back of the room, and realized Peter had leapt up, too. "It's good to see you, Abbie." I threw my arms around the doctor in a giant hug.

Once he was situated in a comfy chair, changed into fresh clothes, and handed a cup of coffee, Dr. Ophellen told us his story. I listened with fascination. "After successfully capturing an adult Weddell seal and giving him a salt lick, I decided I wanted a couple

43

more." *Oh no,* I thought, uneasy. *You should never want 'a couple more'.*

"Anyway, after leaving a note, saying the keys were to be given to Peter Williams and Abbie Forester, I left, taking my snow mobile," the doctor continued. "I left for the place where the sea-ice starts, you know, behind that slope just before you reach the common area. I got my equipment and tried to capture more Weddell seals.

"I managed to grab a minnow-like fish, but no cute, harmless seals, as you call them, Abbie. I decided to move down the sea-ice a little further. I kept moving down, closer and closer to the place where Ross Island breaks off and the ocean stretches ahead of you. I just wanted to get one seal. One seal! It didn't seem like a hard goal, so I kept going. I kept working at the ice, I kept pounding, hoping to see the creature I wanted.

"The sun sank without my noticing. As I said before, I just wanted to get one seal. That was my wish, my motivation, and all I could think of. I couldn't think of the time or how dark it was getting. You two were probably heading to bed. It was around eleven o'clock when I finally realized I had to get home.

"I trudged back in the direction where I came from, but suddenly, a snow storm blew in my path. I practically fell over. I pushed against the winds, crawling on my hands and knees to survive. Up ahead of me, I could see the Human Infractions Studies building, where I knew there were some small dorms. I crawled until I reached the door, pulling it open just before the wind blew so hard that a piece of equipment fell over.

"I stayed there all night, and now, I'm here," Dr. Ophellen finished. I let my jaw gape open at his story. I wouldn't have been able to make it through something like that - me, Abbie Forester, stuck in a blizzard, in Antarctica! No way.

Peter's eyebrows told me that he was equally impressed and worried. "Would you like some more coffee?" he asked the doctor, in a weak voice. Dr. Ophellen laughed, and then nodded his head. He seemed very tired.

"I guess you were unsuccessful," I said, giggling. The doctor beamed a crooked smile at me. I could tell he was glad to be back here, back to his precious lab, back with his friends, scientists or people like Peter and I, back to taking care of Lucky, surrounded by the familiar scenes of McMurdo Station. All of this had to have shaken up the doctor.

The three of us sat in the lab for a while, just relaxing and thinking how glad we were that Dr. Ophellen was safe. I wanted to share the news with my parents, but that could wait a while. I needed to spend some time with the doctor. The scare of not seeing him like that, and having a terrifying story to explain his absence; it had all thrown me off track.

"Well, I guess we should get going," Peter announced finally, after a while of chatting. I stood up and brushed my seat off. After exchanging hugs and 'so-glad-you're-back' glances, I left for the dorm. The trip seemed long and boring. I just wanted to take a personal golf cart back to Building 9.

45

My mom was lying on her cot when I got back. She was snoring away, sound asleep. Dad was sitting next to her, watching some TV. His eyes barely left the screen when he greeted me. "Hey, did you find that doctor?"

"Yes, I found 'that doctor'," I snorted, annoyed. "He was stuck in a snowstorm and had to stay at the Human Infractions Studies building the whole night." That sure caught my father's attention. He sat up a little straighter and faced me, painfully having to take his gaze off the Australian Network.

"That, honey, is a dangerous thing." His face was stone serious, reflecting his serious parent thoughts. "Never get stuck-"

"-in a blizzard alone," I groaned. "I know, Dad. That happened to Dr. Ophellen, not me, okay?" I rolled my eyes and flopped onto my cot. Sure, I'd been there last night, although not necessarily sleeping. I had been awake the entire time, imagining what kind of terrible things Dr. Ophellen was possibly experiencing.

In a couple of quick seconds, I found myself in Dreamland.

I was revving the engine of a quad, stepping on the gas and quickly braking again. When it finally worked, I flew off into the snowy night. The moon shown in my path, guiding my way with a trail of light beams. I kept going, pressing on the pedal, passing Amanda's building, every place I'd been to, really. I passed the Discovery Building, the 'mess hall', the lab, even the Human Infractions Studies building, which I'd never been to. Of course, I was in a dream, so the building wasn't realistic. I caught a glance as

I flew by; it was modern and open and filled with clear windows.

I cut the engine once I reached a hole, a deep pit full of murky blackness. I stepped off the quad, not able to control myself, as if in a trance. I babbled a string of weird words that I seemed to know, but inside, I truly didn't.

Out of the hole came a noise, so loud that if this were but a dream I couldn't bear to hear it. There was Lucky! Something was wrong: she didn't make that much of a racket.

"Lucky?" I asked hesitantly. Suddenly, I saw a red liquid coming from the hole, or maybe even the Weddell seal herself. "Are you... bleeding?" She made the adorable yipping sound she'd made the first time I ever saw her, although this time, it wasn't a cute noise. It was a cry for help.

I tried to reach in and get her out of the stupid hole, but I couldn't. It was like something was holding me back - something didn't want me to save Lucky. "Come on, girlie, you have to work with me here," I told Lucky. I hoped she understood the meaning of those words, and yanked with all my might.

No matter how hard I tried, the dream-me couldn't get Lucky out of that hole. I tried all sorts of different, creative, helpful ways, which didn't work. I tried everything I could possibly imagine; and nothing would get her out.

Suddenly, Lucky was gone. She slipped from my hands, from my sight, from the world. She fell right back into her own blood, and drowned. It was like the story that Dr. Ophellen had told me, when he let the penguin go. With me, I didn't let her go. I hadn't lost hope. But Lucky was truly finished. Truly missing, missing from me.

I woke up, gasping for air, and panting. My mom was leaning over my bed, her thin eyebrows furrowed. "Are you okay, sweetie?" she asked, a concerned tone brushing her voice. I nodded and smiled a fragile smile.

"Just a bad dream," I said weakly. "It's nothing, really." I had to insist this because my dad had joined Mom in her sympathetic act of standing above me and patting my hand. I got up slowly, walked over to the bathroom, and got a wet washcloth. I rubbed it over the sweat that was dripping off my forehead, in an attempt to clean it off.

"Scary dreams are a part of growing up," my mother said approvingly. "You know that, right, Abbie?" I sighed. I swerved my head from side to side, as if trying to shake everything off me. I grabbed some cozy sweats and a camp t-shirt, and put them on in the bathroom after splashing some water on my face.

My parents had respectfully moved away from my bed and were back to their TV-watching on the other cot, still eyeing me as if to make sure I was okay. I pulled out my book and read for a while. It seemed to calm me down a bit; I stopped shaking.

Lucky is fine, I thought, reassuring myself. *You need to relax. Take a deep breath. In. Out. In. Out.* I managed to get my respiration back to normal, and my heartbeat at a reasonable pace. I continued to read until it was dinnertime. I put on some thicker clothes silently and followed my parents to the dining hall.

"Has anyone gone on the Climate Change Expedition?" my dad asked, once our family had joined the rest of the scientists, on their way to the evening meal. "It was absolutely incredible. Truly amazing." Nobody nodded their head, so I guessed Dad had been the only one to go on the trek. It was probably boring; if the other scientists didn't want to go because the expedition was dreary, my dad was definitely there.

"I've been!" a sassy voice chirped. A feeling of dread filled my stomach. I knew whose voice that belonged to. It was horrible, terrible Amanda. I turned around, as did everyone else, to face the menace of the dark side. There she was, dressed in a tight, gold ski suit, and some *very* high-heeled shoes, especially for a scientist. "It's wonderful, I'll give you that one. I mean, the professor? Absolutely incredible, Dr. Forester. He was so adorable!"

I had originally thought Amanda meant that the professor was a fantastic teacher with incredible descriptions, a great expedition leader, but now I knew: she was shallow. She was simply into fashion when she should have focused on being a scientist. She was into cute guys when she should have been focused on research at McMurdo. It disgusted me.

"Do you mean adorable as in gorgeous? Or as in a very intelligent scientist?" I snapped back, a bit snooty. Well, Amanda sure deserved it. She was a no-good beast with a passion for girly stuff, instead of a care for preserving the environment and scientific exploration.

"E-excuse me?" she chirped, flushing. I was about to reply

49

with something quite arrogant, but a look from my mom told me to shut my mouth. I did. We trudged the rest of the way to the dining hall. I enjoyed the smug silence with much pleasure. It meant that Amanda had to be quiet, too, which she wasn't very good at doing.

I didn't feel like eating much, so all I got was a pesto salad and some delicious tea. I looked over at Amanda's tray, which was heaped to the brim with my same meal, except for the tea was replaced with a mocha. I rolled my eyes.

"I've got really bad news." I looked up to see Peter standing over me, not dressed in his usual flannel outfit and beanie cap. He was in official winter gear, the parka, the snow pants, and the furry boots. Peter's eyebrows were scrunched in a worried pose.

"What -" I barely had time to say anything before he was rushing me away from my confused parents. "We'll be back in ten!" I shouted over my shoulder as I was pulled out the front door, into the night, and all the way to Dr. Ophellen's lab. I gasped for a breath when I finally went through the door.

The doctor was pacing back and forth, biting his fingers and mumbling something unintelligible. I looked at Peter, questioning this behavior. He simply led me to the table where Dr. Ophellen had first examined Lucky and pointed to a note.

I know what you're doing. Stop right now. It's illegal. You can't help animals like that. It's against the laws of nature, how the earth has been since the beginning of time. You can't change the facts in encyclopedias. Or the laws of nature. Weddell seals will continue to only live up to 20 years. They'll stay like that. If they don't, you're going to pay. You're going to pay, big time. Stop right now, just like I told you. I don't think you want a personal visit from me.

"Who would do something like that?" I cried out after reading the crumpled piece of paper. "And, most importantly, who would know about Mission Lucky?" I stood there, examining the note, wondering about anybody who could have written anything so horrible. Amanda - she probably wouldn't have a clue if the world were coming to an end, she'd be more focused on fixing her lipstick. I couldn't think of anyone else besides her. I was officially stumped.

"I'm going to investigate," Peter told me firmly, his eyes changing into slits. "I'm going to find out who wrote that stupid note, and destroy them!" He pounded his fist on the table with a bang. It was so loud that Dr. Ophellen came rushing over, only to slump his shoulders again. The doctor clearly was upset about this whole fiasco.

"First, we'll have to make a list," I decided. I marched over to Dr. Ophellen's computer, opened a blank document, and wrote down a lot of people, doctors, and scientists at the McMurdo Station. I put a blank check box next to each name, which would be either checked, question marked, or eliminated. Most of the good-natured scientists would be eliminated from the list of the potential dark, evil-type.

I printed out three copies of the list: one for me, one for

Peter, and of course, one for Dr. Ophellen. I handed out pens, and sat down at the table, almost like an official editor of a magazine. "We need to start at the beginning of the list," I said. "So that would be... Dr. Donner."

Peter shook his head. "Dr. Donner is a very kind man. He helped me load up some heavy supplies the other day, and he loves animals. I don't think he'd ever do something so terrible as this." I nodded and eliminated his name off my list. I waited for everyone to scratch their pens as well.

"Alright, now... Dr. Enrico," I continued. I gazed over at Peter's expression. It was questioning and blank. I could tell he didn't know who Dr. Enrico was. I didn't know him very well either; it was my dad who talked about the doctor one day.

"He's a little suspicious," Dr. Ophellen said, finally ending the silence. "He doesn't like me that much, either, so if Dr. Enrico found out, it could be possible that he'd threaten me." I put a question mark next to the name, and added a note that said to investigate the man.

I went through the entire list with Peter and Dr. Ophellen, putting a check or question mark by each name. There were about fourteen out of the fifty names that were labeled suspicious, which was a pretty good score. Now we could narrow everything down much easier. I split jobs of investigating between us all, then thanked the two guys and rushed back to the dining hall.

"What was that all about?" my mom asked hopefully, wiggling her eyebrows. She and Dad were still under the impression that Peter was my boyfriend. I just had to get that impression erased.

"Dr. Ophellen had an emergency at the lab," I explained. "Since Peter is extremely good friends with the doctor, and Dr. Ophellen is also a fantastic friend to me, he wanted me to come help as well." My dad and mom sighed quietly, nodding and exchanging expressions of defeat to one another. We finished our meal, then headed back to Building 9.

I did my usual happy dance when Mom checked the mail. It had finally arrived, the first time after the two weeks we'd been here. I received five letters. Two were from my best friend back in Taiwan, with a detailed description of all her experiences with her many brothers, sisters, grandmothers, and relatives; another from my aunt Alise, telling me how she missed me and wanted me to come visit her in Michigan; one was actually a catalogue from my favorite clothing brand; and finally, a exceedingly gigantic letter from a girl I'd met in London, when my mom and I had been there while my dad was studying sleet in France (very boring, we both decided). Her name was Emily, and she was a really nice 'lassie', as the people would say where she was from.

"Well, aren't you Miss Popular." Dad proclaimed. I blushed and ran up the stairs, still reading the last few paragraphs in Emily's letter. Once I got into the dorm, I took time to sit down and write back to all my friends, even including ol' aunt Alise. I circled a few things in the catalogue, but I couldn't order anything here in Antarctica. The company made spring and summer clothing, which I could not wear in this freezing snow and wind.

"'Night, guys," I told my parents when I got into bed, already yawning. It had been a long day, full of Amanda and worries and stress. I just wanted to relax. My mom and dad probably said 'goodnight' back, although I couldn't hear them. I was already asleep.

When I got out of bed the next day, I checked the alarm clock, finding it was exactly eleven thirty, and that my parents had left me another one of their annoying notes. It explained that they had gone to send out the letters, eat some breakfast, and that they would be back soon, bringing a meal-in-bed for me.

Their kind gesture made me suspicious. "Interesting," I muttered. I sat there for a while, with the TV on mute, staring out the window at the snow. It was coming down in hard clumps now, spreading itself like a blanket over the volcanic rock that covered the McMurdo Station. Some snowflakes slid down the windows, reminding of the first time I'd ever come here.

After truly waking up, I got dressed and checked my "to-investigate" list. My *first* choice, Amanda. I grinned a sly smile. With one continuous move, I hopped off the cot, raced down the stairs, and burst into the cold morning. The wind brushed my cheeks gently, but it stung as though it had slapped me, not brushed.

I ran down the sloped hill and straight across the shoveled path to Amanda's building. The heaters warmed me up, however, they couldn't prevent the excitement in my chest from bubbling up through my mouth. "Is Amanda here?" I called into the open space. I could hear the familiar clicking of the same high-heels as the suspect

54

walked into plain sight.

"Oh, it's you," she said, her nose pinched as if I was something odorous under her nose. She fixed her sloppy bun by poking a pen into it, and then returned her attention to me; the pungent object she was *forced* to take care of. "So? Whaddaya want?" She slurred 'what', 'do', and 'you' together in one messy word. It reminded me of a lesson taught by incredible Mrs. Bower, my fifth grade teacher: 'never use slang words to make up for real ones'. Amanda needed desperately to go back to grade school!

"I've come to interview you," I lied. I had practiced this for a while with Peter. I was ready for show time. "It's going to be for a project, you know, since I'm home-schooled." This was partially true, but here in Antarctica, my mother had, for some strange reason, decided I could take a break. I guess this counted as a Christmas vacation, since it was so snowy.

"That's great! Thank you so much for choosing me to interview," Amanda squealed, clapping her manicured hands together. The smacking noise echoed around the building awkwardly. I stared at her for a second, contemplating her strength. *I could beat her at Friday Night Boxing, back when we stayed in Kentucky*, I thought, convinced.

"Well, let's start with the first question," I said, matter-of-factly, once we'd sat down in the chairs. I decided not to take the beanbag, or else Amanda would be suspicious about how serious I really was. "'What is it like to be a scientist at one of America's research stations?'"

Amanda chewed on the pencil she'd just pulled out of her hair, trying hard to think of an answer to the simple question. "The McMurdo Station is a fascinating place, really," she replied finally. "We have a lot of fantastic scientists here, and a whole lot of research that we do. I love researching, you know, especially about climate and geography." I nodded, pretending to be interested. I wrote down her response on my sheet of paper.

"Okay... 'If a fellow scientist was caught doing something that was against the rules, what would your reaction be?'" I knew the question was a bit risky, but I could, in fact, risk it. Amanda couldn't do anything too serious; after all, I was merely thirteen! I used my age as an advantage.

"I wouldn't report anything to the officials until I let the person know how wrong it is to do such a thing." Amanda replied quite quickly, disturbing me. I scribbled down her answer on the piece of paper, taking a small amount of time to do so, hoping she wouldn't notice how excited I was. Amanda was *definitely* going in the "Highly Suspicious" category.

"Actually, I find this is the last question, since I have to interview other scientists with the same questions!" I announced. I raised my eyebrows in fake surprise. "Here it is - 'tell us one memorable experience in your career as a scientist'." I made that one up on the fly. I had to do something she wouldn't think much of; something she'd know was normal.

"I think maybe when I discovered a patch of ice that was only a few feet deep, in a cluster with others that were all at least fifty feet! It was incredible. I even received an award for doing amazing work with a 3D depth measurement." I was actually interested in that. I wrote it down, thanked Amanda, and flew out of there as quickly as possible. I couldn't wait to show Peter and Dr. Ophellen the results.

I bumped into my mom and another woman scientist on my way to the lab. She giggled and whispered to her newly found friend. "This is Savannah, but you should probably call her Dr. Chang," my mom announced, nudging her. They burst out into a fit of laughter, so I just nodded my head awkwardly and rushed away.

Once I *finally* reached Dr. Ophellen's lab, I scrambled inside, still gasping for air. Peter looked up, surprised, from the book he was reading. I didn't give him a glance before marching over to Dr. Ophellen, who was sitting at his desk, hard at work. "I've 'interviewed' Amanda, and I think she might be a prime suspect!" I panted. I shoved the paper in front of the doctor and let him read.

Dr. Ophellen took a long time to read everything I'd recorded, looking over everything twice. I sighed impatiently, waiting for him to finish. I rolled my eyes when he finished. "This is true, Abbie," he said, looking up from his glasses. "Amanda seems like she could definitely threaten me with a note like the one on my desk. But I'm sure we'll have to wait and see the results from the other doctors." I sighed again.

Peter simply kept his eyebrows up, high on top of his forehead, showing how surprised he was at my enthusiasm. I glared at him (he deserved it; he had been ignorant and rude to me), then turned around, showing my anger towards the two men in the lab. How could they not see? Amanda truly had written the note, without any doubt!

"You can't falsely accuse someone," Peter told me, breaking the tense silence. I didn't turn around but stopped in my tracks, on my way out of the door. "Amanda is probably only an extremely horrible woman, an extremely messed-up person, and an evil creature who's out to get you!"

"Very helpful," I growled. I sighed and adjusted my hair into a sloppy bun, although not really wanting to imitate the dark Amanda's hairstyle. "Really, guys. Please take me seriously. I know Amanda is the one who did this." I waited for them to realize they were wrong, waited for them to apologize until I smirked, and told them to stop. But they didn't. Peter and Dr. Ophellen simply exchanged a know-it-all glanced. They returned to their previous activities without a care in the world. "Excuse me?! Hello?"

I marched out of the door, steam coming out from my ears a million miles per second. I couldn't believe it. My two best of best friends, completely ignoring me. How could they? Amanda truly was guilty. I knew it for a fact, in my gut I knew it and so should Dr. Ophellen and Peter.

"Stupid, stupid boys," I muttered to myself, as the whipping wind stung my face and the snow poured down from the black sky. The dorms were just ahead of me, but I didn't step inside Building 9. I just stared across the way, looking across at the place where I knew Amanda lurked, evil surrounding her like a dark cloak. What a cruel person she was!

With reluctance, I went up the stairs, still sulking, to my dorm room. A mug of hot chocolate was resting on my bedside 'table', which was more like just a makeshift chair. I grinned and took a drink from the cup. It tasted delicious, as always…I wondered who'd left it there.

"Hey, honey!" a voice crowed. I looked up from the drink to see my mom, flouncing in through the door. She plopped down on my cot. "Did you like it? Of course, hot cocoa was Savannah's idea." I nodded, as if it there was, of course, only one possibility; that Savannah always came up the thought of giving me a delicious beverage. I, naturally, was just delighted to have some hot chocolate.

"So, what about that breakfast you and Dad were thinking about giving me?" I asked, trying to sound casual. I knew something was up, although I couldn't quite put a finger on the actual reason. "Did you want to talk?"

My mom opened her mouth, then shut it again. She lowered her eyes down on the bed, and squeezed them shut, as if thinking of what to say. Finally, Mom lifted her head back up again. "Your father, since he's almost finished with his study - Abbie, I don't know - how to explain - this situation." She broke off a lot, her voice stiff and brittle. "Look, sweetie, there's something we have to say. Dad is pretty much done here, at the McMurdo Station, you know. After this month is over, I think it'll be time to move on."

I gasped at the mere mention of even *thinking* of leaving here. All right, sure, we did move around from place to place almost every three months, like nomads, hopping from place to place and never settling down. But vanishing forever from the place I loved, the place where I had an animal I loved-- was impossible. No way!

"Mom, you can't do this," I whispered, tracing my finger along the edge of my blanket. The design curled around in swirls, slowly weaving across the cot. I wouldn't be able to ever see this again, once we'd packed up like we always did, and moved to some other place. "Besides, where else is there to go?" I forced out a cold laugh. "We've practically been everywhere."

Even with my last question unanswered, the dorm remained silent. It kept quiet for three minutes, four, five, six- about twenty long, quiet minutes passed before I actually heard someone's breath. It was my father, huffing his way into the room. "Oh hey, guys!" His cheerful tone cut off when he saw my incredibly mad expression set into my face, and my mother's pleading look, complete with her mastered doe eyes.

My family all sat together on my bed. "Please reconsider this," I begged, finally. "I have to stay here for a while longer. Just a little while." My mom sighed and patted Dad's hand. The glove met hers with a loud smack, but I didn't even jump.

"A month is a little while, Abbie," my dad said. "You know you can't get attached to any place. Antarctica is wonderful. It is absolutely gorgeous, stunning, fascinating, I know that. Even so, I cannot stay here forever. I have to keep going along with the science program, keep studying climate in other places."

I felt betrayed, hurt. Here were Peter and Dr. Ophellen, not believing me when I knew for a fact Amanda truly had written the nasty note. Here were my mom and dad, my own parents, not listening to me when I asked for, yes, a few more months. Maybe another year. Couldn't they all see? Antarctica was incredible. I still had much to do here, including saving Lucky, making more friends, putting Amanda in her rightful place. There were so many Band-Aids I hand to put on things. Was I not entitled to do so?

"You only care about studying." I spit my words out like lava coming from an erupting volcano. "That's the truth. Don't deny it, *Dr. Forester*. What about me, huh? Don't *I* matter? Doesn't what *I* care about, what *I* believe in, what *I* need to fix, what *I* need to do, does that matter? To *me*, yes. But to *you*?"

"Darling, for one, stop exaggerating so much," my mom sighed, complaining. She said it in an arpeggio, making it go up a sigh, down to an actual sentence. Dad nodded wisely. Of course because he was a scientist, because he could nod wisely, because he made every, single, tiny, minuscule decision for our family. I felt my face grow hot with disgust. "And, dear, you really do matter to us. You're our daughter. You're our little - "

"Yeah, just like how Lucky is my daughter, my little angel," I interrupted. "She matters to me, as well. I let her have food. I let her have... well, when she was still here." I added the last part hastily and pretended to be sad. After taking acting lessons back when we were in Rome, I was very proficient at drama. I squeezed a small tear out of my eye. It tickled as it rolled down my cheek.

My mom gently patted my thigh. "If this is about Lucky,

61

you really shouldn't by crying, Abbie. She's safe right now. Dr. Ophellen took care of her can't you see that? Please stop worrying about everything." My dad and mom sighed a heavy sigh. They gave me some space, no doubt hoping I wouldn't blow my top again. I silently got changed into my pajamas then slipped under the covers, clutching *Wuthering Heights* like it was my savior. I read, letting the hours drift by like clouds on a lazy afternoon sky.

When it was time for the mess hall, my dad tentatively asked, "Are you joining us?" He got his answer immediately, with a firm shake of my head. "Okay. I'll bring you back some food." My parents crept away as fast as they could from my cot. I snorted. Was I some kind of wild animal? A beast? Probably to them! A cold, unchanging mood washed over me.

I was going to prove I belonged here, at the McMurdo Station.

I was going to show Dr. Ophellen and Peter I was right.

I was going to give Amanda a HUGE lecture.

And most importantly, I was going to save Lucky.

Chapter Four

My first step in The Plan was to prove I truly did deserve to stay in Antarctica, here, at the wonderful, terrific McMurdo Station. In order to do so, I decided that 'community service' was a very nice way to show this to my parents. Of course, this type of community service wasn't for free; I was going to get paid.

One day, a week after the big fight, I walked up to Josh. He was still wearing his work outfit, but he wasn't doing his job. Of course, Josh wasn't lazy at all, it was simply break time. I noticed that Ivan was a poor, dirty mess. "Did you get stuck today?" I asked sympathetically. I could always tell when Ivan got stuck.

"Yeah," Josh replied, his eyes sagging. He took a bite of his sandwich, slumping his shoulders down. "I hope I don't get fired." I cocked my head to one side, my idea still clicking its last gears into place before I actually vocalized it aloud.

"Well, you definitely won't get booted if I help you wash Ivan," I grinned. I pulled out, from a big pocket in my parka, an already-wet, gigantic sponge, two rolls of paper towels, and a lot of soap. Josh smiled back at me.

"You can have the job for fifty bucks," he said. "As long as you get this whole big guy." I could just imagine myself going up to my mom, or dad, and showing them that fat wad of bills Josh held in his outstretched hand. I nodded.

"Deal!" I answered quickly. We shook hands to confirm it, and then I got to work. I started with the front of Ivan, wiping the grime off the window, and polishing it to the last sparkling millimeter. I scraped the squashed bugs away, one by one. I got the sides, as well, which took a long time. I scrubbed off the melting snow, the dirt, the filth, the grunge. I worked until the red paint and the white paint practically gleamed. Once I was done with this thing, I was betting Josh would raise my pay to at least a hundred dollars.

The back was easy, so I finished it off in no time. I stepped back to look at Ivan - shining like a star. Josh gave me a gigantic grin. "You earned it all," he told me, handing me a large stack of money. "Keep the change." I winked at him and skipped off, ready to show my parents.

I found them, standing along side a couple of other scientists and chatting. They were outside a building I'd seen a few times, although I wasn't quite sure what actually went on in there. Now I knew: grown-up social time. "Oh, hey, Abbie," my dad said cautiously. He waved to invite me to come over.

"Hey, Dad," I replied, smoothly. "So, Ivan got stuck in the snow today, and I just happened to walk by when Josh had a lunch break. I cleaned the *entire* bus, you know. Look what Josh paid me!" I cheerfully showed him the large lump of crisp money. My dad's eyes widened at the sight. His mouth was glued shut.

My mother walked over to join our small group, eyeing the

cash I held in my hand. She didn't say anything, exactly following in my dad's actions. Finally, the true person she was burst through, and Mom had to comment about my earnings. "Oh, wow, darling! How incredible!" she squealed, fingering the paper. "However did you earn it?"

I rolled my eyes. "I washed Ivan. Yes, the whole thing." My mom said nothing, watching the money like she had before. It was as if she was muttering, *of course she didn't steal it... but no, we're still moving out of here*. My heart sank when her half-smile turned to a wobbly line.

"Honey, we have to-"

"Mom, we've been over this before. I am clearly not happy with your decision or Dad's, either. I feel like you are being extremely inconsiderate of my feelings, and only taking yours into account," I told her calmly. I used my vocabulary as a point earner for my mother's "Can Abby Stay?" catalogue.

She raised her eyebrows, saying nothing me. I folded the money with a satisfying crinkle into my pocket, and watched as the chatting continued, with my dad laughing loudly in one corner, adults grabbing more crackers, everything calm... except for where my mom and I stood awkwardly.

"I know we've discussed it," Mom said finally. She cleared her throat. "I've talked with your father, and we decided that since you have really been diligent about helping Dr. Ophellen in the lab, and all the other things you've dedicated your time to here... I think the Foresters might be able to spend another month in Antarctica!"

I squealed in delight and hugged my mom first, then rushed over to squeeze my dad. They were both so nice! So kind! So generous! All right, I might not have thought that before, but my mom had changed my mind. I smiled again, making sure my parents got the point that this was the best decision they'd ever made.

It was the truth, because now I could set everything right. I could help prove to Peter and Dr. Ophellen that I was right about my suspicions, and I could see Lucky off when she was ready to become an independent, and healthy, Weddell seal. And of course, there was Amanda to deal with.

"Thank you," I barely managed to say. "I promise - I'll show you that I deserve this extra month." My mom nodded, like it was okay, like nothing big had happened. She turned and continued to laugh with the other grown-ups. *That's my mom*, I thought, smiling.

On my way to the lab, I thought of an organized, well-presented speech I could give to Peter and Dr. Ophellen. I pretended I was the President, speaking about Amanda being guilty, even though my audience wasn't exactly enthusiastic about the idea. It was a hard task to even get their attention, for starters.

Peter was still engrossed in his book, eyes wide open as he gobbled in each word. Dr. Ophellen was hard at work, muttering and clicking buttons on his computer. I made a coughing noise so they would notice me.

"Hello there, Abbie," Dr. Ophellen said stiffly. I could tell he was still a bit hurt about my reaction to his simple, peacemaker response to my clear evidence about Amanda. He took a step closer to where I stood, and reached out to hand me a cup of something hot and steamy. I presumed it was cocoa; therefore, I shook my head to tell him I didn't want any.

"If you don't think that Amanda wrote that note, I don't blame you," I began. When Peter sighed and tried to interrupt, I held up my hand, closing my eyes at the same time. I'd seen many people (official, business-like people) do this, and it was an official, business-like maneuver. "However, the proof is clear, and the evidence is unmistakably true. Amanda *is* the one who did this. You have to hear me out, both of you. Just try."

Peter was silent for a long time, scratching the stubs on his chin and contemplating everything I'd said, but Dr. Ophellen hesitated only for a few moments, before nodding to show his consent. "I'm sorry I doubted you," he apologized. "Forgive me. You are right. Amanda must have written that terrible note."

I smiled at him with tight, sealed lips then turned my gaze over to the always-unsure Peter. He was jiggling his leg, flushing nervously, showing signs that he knew that yes, I was right. Like always. "Y-ye-yeah, you're right, Abbie," he said quickly. "Sorry. Amanda? She's guilty. Totally." I laughed and told him I forgave him.

Now, almost everything in The Plan was finished, except for giving a huge talk to my horrible, horrific, terrible archenemy, and 'saving' Lucky. I hadn't been paying much attention to her those days, just stopping by to give a quick wave, or a grin, or a 'hello'. However, I hadn't known at the time what Lucky was doing, how well she was faring, all the things I should have been paying attention to.

The next day, everything changed. It seemed like an innocent morning; I ate my usual breakfast, bundled up in fewer clothes since the weather was changing since summer was arriving, and ran to the lab. I had come up with a plan - one that involved Peter confronting Amanda. I couldn't wait to tell the doctor and Peter.

"Hey, how's-" I broke off from my cheerful greeting when I noticed Dr. Ophellen sulking in the corner. He wasn't busy doing his usual research, he was simply, well, sulking. He was hunched up, face stony, and eyes red.

"It's Lucky." Dr. Ophellen's voice sounded tired, strained. He turned to look at me and I saw the worry etched on his skin. "She hasn't been feeling well, and I think she might have gotten sick to the stomach, perhaps an effect of the salt blocks." I gasped. The idea of the mineral licks had seemed perfect, not able to be broken, not able to fail.

"Has that happened to any of the other Weddell seals you've been giving the nutrients to?" I asked immediately. Surely, if it affected Lucky, it affected others of her kind. However, Dr. Ophellen shook his head in answer.

"No, only Lucky," he told me. "The rest of them have been absolutely fine. It's only your little girl who's gotten her stomach upset from the salt blocks." I grinned. I liked the way he called Lucky my 'little girl', although the rest of his news report wasn't anything to smile about. What if we couldn't save my darling seal?

The rest of the day definitely did not escalate from there. My dad wasn't feeling well; he had a stuffy nose and a cough, my mom told me she might have to rethink the extra month on account of my father's illness, Dr. Rose left on Ivan to go back home, because her sister had just died from cancer, and Peter wouldn't talk to me when I visited him at the supply building. He was deeply concerned about Lucky, although he didn't want to share his troubles with anyone else.

I went to the dorm, murmuring condolences to myself, trying to make myself more at ease. *Maybe I should just leave*, I thought at one point, although I quickly changed my mind about that. A good dose of reading seemed inviting, so I pulled out my worn novel and finished off three thick chapters.

However, *Wuthering Heights* didn't do me much good. I finally decided that drawing would help relieve some stress. I pulled out my sketchbook with the intention of portraying my sadness that Lucky wasn't healing, but then a new idea popped into my head: I could write a note back to Amanda!

Amanda-

I wish I could say 'thank you' for the little letter I received from you a couple days ago, although given what you told me in the note. I, regrettably, cannot express my gratitude. What I am doing is not illegal; I am simply boosting their strength so the species can continue to thrive. You need to calm down, please, and perhaps rethink what you believe I am doing.

You may or may not respond, that doesn't concern me. What concerns me is why you think my caring actions are against the law.

Once I'd drafted the note enough to think it was absolutely perfect, I walked over to the building Amanda resided in, and left the letter in an official envelope addressed to her. I left quietly, praying nobody noticed I'd paid a little visit to Amanda.

If they saw me, I was dead. And so was Dr. Ophellen.

As my boots pounded against the snow while I ran, heart beating to the same rhythm, I swore I could hear Lucky cry out for help. I tried plugging my ears; it didn't help one bit. Even with my hands pressed against the flaps and crevices of my ears, Lucky's yelps were as audible as ever.

I ran to the lab, hoping that Lucky's heart was still beating, steadily as ever. I sighed in relief when I saw she was swimming around the aquarium, a little sad, but happy to see me nonetheless. I pressed my sticky fingers against the glass, smiling and wishing I could pet Lucky, like I did when I first saw her.

"She's stable, although not getting better very fast," Dr. Ophellen boomed above me. I turned away from the aquarium to see him standing in the corner next to me. He was holding a clipboard in one hand, a pen in the other, and was writing things, probably information and observations about how Lucky was doing. He showed me Lucky's pulse monitor, and the status seemed steady again.

"Will she ever recover from the overdose of minerals?" I

asked, concerned. "Lucky seems a little... less enthusiastic, I guess." Dr. Ophellen nodded. We both knew that she could be very hyper when she was happy, and now she clearly wasn't happy at all.

I stayed there for a while, constantly checking on Lucky and reviewing the clipboard. Nothing was improving, but nothing was getting worse. I watched Peter come in, look at Lucky, and leave. The sun set and Dr. Ophellen told me to go back to my dorm, since it was getting late.

"I'll stay here," I whispered, still holding my gaze on Lucky. I hoped, I prayed she would get better, or else this whole month that my parents allowed me would go to waste. I really needed Lucky. I wished that Lucky could see that, I wished it would give her the courage to hang on.

Suddenly, an outline of a faint idea came to me. I went onto Dr. Ophellen's computer and began to research vitamins and sodium and salt blocks very quickly. My fingers were like lightning as I clicked on the buttons. Finally, I came to the same page that had given me the information about mineral licks at the beginning.

"'Some animals may have a reaction to certain ingredients in salt blocks,'" I read from the page. I moaned. *Great. Why couldn't they have put this warning at the top of the page people read first?* "They can have an upset stomach, headache, fever, or abnormal blood pressure as a response to specific ingredients for mineral licks. To cure minor cases of these symptoms, and depending on the animal, of course, you should give the animal a...." The website listed a bunch of pills that might cure the symptoms.

I wanted to tell Peter immediately, and ask him if the supply building carried any of the vitamins, but everything was closing just around the time I logged off the computer. I sighed; my plan would have to continue the next day.

Back at the dorm, my mom and dad were watching the news on their cot, with worried and crazed looks displayed on their faces. The Australian Network was on, the light blaring onto the back wall. I quickly padded over to where they were frozen, their eyes glued to the screen.

"Tony Antellio, a revered meteorologist, predicts that there will be a *huge* snowstorm in a small part of Antarctica. The place is called the McMurdo Sound, home to the McMurdo Station. Here is Tony, explaining what might happen if his prediction comes true." I watched the perky newscaster wave a little bit, and the screen transferred to a blurry clip of a bearded guy in cargo pants and a leather jacket.

Tony coughed, which sounded like a mouse squeak on the poor recording equipment. "Yeah, if the blizzard comes, it'll be real hard on the people who work at McMurdo," he said. I couldn't see how Tony could be 'revered'. He didn't seem much like a meteorologist, either. "There'll be so much snow that all the machines will have to stop running. The expeditions, research missions, everything will be forced to close down temporarily."

The TV shut off and my mom just looked at me, half-smiling. "This probably is going to happen. You'll just have to be prepared for it, Abbie. If the snowstorm indeed occurs, it'll delay us at least for a few weeks."

I nodded, but didn't really pay attention to her warnings. I only cared about Lucky. She wouldn't be affected by the snowstorm after all; she was safe inside the incredible aquarium. Lucky was simply affected by the salt blocks, something that was supposed to make her stronger, and I had to make sure she'd get better.

"Goodnight, sweetie," my dad and mom said in unison, and turned off their light. I watched them crawl under the covers, their only worry a minor one, at least minuscule compared to mine.

"Goodnight," I replied, my voice echoing around the dorm room. I stared out into the dark night long after I heard snores coming from the bed next to me. I couldn't sleep at all.

The next day, I couldn't wait to get out of bed. I got dressed as quickly as I possibly could, and then raced to where Peter was working. I'd promised him I would help him shelve things, and I also wanted to tell him about the medicines that might help Lucky.

"What's gotten into you?" Peter asked me suspiciously, as I ran into the supply 'shack'. It had become very shabby ever since Peter had neglected even *trying* to arrange things in order.

"Just - just happy," I giggled, trying to look flouncy and dreamy. Peter shook his head and went back to shelving some packages haphazardly. I sat on a cask of something, waiting for him to finish. We had plans to eat dinner with Dr. Ophellen that night, and to discuss what options Lucky had.

"And Peter?" I said. He looked up from a heavy crate of empty vials. "I wanted to know if you had some of these medications..." I listed out some of the medicines from the website that I'd recorded in my small sketchbook, and it turned out, the supply shack did carry a couple.

Once Peter was finally finished with his job, I grabbed him by the hand and pulled him out into the snow, clutching a bag of various vials, tubes, and syringes. We ran all the way to the lab, where a delicious smell of microwavable dinner was wafting through the windows. I smiled. *It must be Dr. Ophellen's favorite heat-up pot roast and Mrs. Smith's cherry pie*, I thought.

"Welcome!" Dr. Ophellen cried when we stepped in the door. All around us were some snowflake decorations, streamers, and balloons. Dr. Ophellen had put a plastic table in one corner. He'd set it with some cheap knifes and forks, and blue, shiny cups. I grinned.

"This is perfect, Dr. Ophellen," I told him truthfully. Peter simply nodded his agreement. He was practically already eating by the time the doctor and I were barely getting seated.

I helped myself to the delectable pot roast, potatoes, and carrots. The smell was mouthwatering; I couldn't resist seconds. Several servings later, I leaned back in my chair, deciding I couldn't eat any more of the main course. I needed my dessert!

The cherry pie tasted just like it had back when we were moving all around the Midwest region of America; it was sweet, smooth, with the perfect glossy flavor. I remembered having it with my friend Susie, and Carter, and all my other pals back there. It brought a wave of comfort to me.

"Thank you so much," I said, Peter echoing me. We chatted with Dr. Ophellen for a while about the McMurdo Station's latest scandal about another doctor, and everyone agreed the gossip was complete insanity. The talk was lighthearted until we settled down to business, and got out our clipboards.

I marked off the check boxes next to our three names to record our attendance, then turned back to face my small audience. "Hello, thank you for joining the fifteenth successful Saving Lucky meeting," I said formally. There was a polite round of applause before I quieted Peter and Dr. Ophellen. "Lucky seems to be getting slightly better, although, doctor, you'll have to confirm this is true."

"Her blood pressure is back down to normal, and she hasn't gotten sick in the past few days," Dr. Ophellen verified. "Lucky is pulling through quite well."

I beamed at the announcement and snuck a glance over at my favorite little Weddell seal. She was swimming around in circles, seeming more like her happy, confident self.

"Thank you, boys, please write a note about this improvement," I instructed. I watched as the pencils scratched on the white pieces of paper. I doodled a heart with wings while waiting for Peter and Dr. Ophellen to finish taking notes. "It has come to my concern that the number of Weddell seals we successfully strengthen every week has been decreased. Do we need more assistance?"

Peter raised his hand like I was the teacher and I nodded impatiently. "With only one person able to sneak salt blocks from the building, only one person to help run this whole operation, and only one person who can actually catch those seals, it's hard to make Saving Lucky easy," Peter said. "If we can find someone we can trust, I say we hire them."

I raised my eyebrows. It was a good idea. After all, there were plenty of people we could trust to keep Lucky's secret at McMurdo, and Saving Lucky could make more progress if there were a couple more folks helping out with catching seals and sneaking salt blocks and helping to piece everything together.

"Take Peter's idea into account under the 'Worthy Ideas' section of your page, please," I instructed. Again, I heard the familiar scratching of pencil against paper, and dozed off in a daydream of flowers, sunshine, and Lucky.

I decided it was time to show Dr. Ophellen the medicines. When I pulled out my bag, and retold the information I had discovered, his eyes lit up in delight. "Fantastic work, Abigail!" he cried out, making me flush. It wasn't a huge accomplishment; he could have easily done it himself. Still, I was proud that I'd found something that would be able to help the adorable Weddell seal.

After that, we went over a few more subjects, like the price of salt blocks, and whether or not to confront Amanda, things such as those. I made a mental note to 'interview' a few more scientists here.

I walked back to the dorm, smiling to myself. Peter and Dr. Ophellen were respecting me, just like they should have when I told them about Amanda. Well, they hadn't respected me then... look where it had gotten them!

I changed into my pajamas and tried to read for a while. My eyelids felt heavy on my eyes; lead on my eyeballs. I closed my eyes and felt a world of refreshment crash over me.

That night, plans of more and more things to do swirled in my head. I was glad to be asleep, but even then, the exhaustion of everything still lingered with me... the extra month was going to be a long one.

Chapter Five

I stepped into the building cautiously, scanning the room, looking for a person anywhere. I'd been unsuccessful with my mission to find a few extra helpers for Saving Lucky, and I was desperate to change that status.

"Hello?" I called into the empty place. My voice echoed off the walls and bounced back to me. I shuddered. I'd never been to this part of the McMurdo Station before, even when I took the tour with Dr. Smith, and it looked quite forlorn.

"Oh, please come in," a woman answered. I stepped up to the desk in the empty room. There was a young lady sitting there, dressed in furry clothing. She was shutting down her computer, probably getting ready to leave her shift. It was the Welcoming and Information Services, which wasn't visited much, by the looks of it, at least.

"There's something I've asked a few people here," I began nervously. I couldn't do the fake interview excuse anymore, since my mom had blabbed to everyone that I had an 'academical break' at the moment. "Can-can you keep a secret?"

"I can," the woman said, smiling. "I kept it a secret that my boss left on a two month trip to Japan so she could visit her family. I

78

even pretended to be her. I took acting before I decided I wanted to be an assistant helper here."

"Well..." I explained Dr. Ophellen's whole story, about Lucky, Peter, Amanda, basically the story of everyone who was involved with the project, in a helpful or not way. I made sure to tell her that I was looking for some extra helpers, some people who would be able to help us run the system more easily.

The woman was surprised at my tale, probably thinking something about my astoundingly young age, and incredibly mature quest. Saving Lucky was indeed something that could be shocking.

"Of course!" she exclaimed after only a few moments, wiping the old expression off her face, then replacing it with happiness. "By the way, my name is Sue Ling." From then on, I knew her as Sue, the miracle worker.

It wasn't an overstatement at all. Sue Ling proved she could help with Dr. Ophellen's job, catching Weddell seals with her lightning-quick reflexes to jump up and grab a seal from the water, just as it popped up for air. She could also assist Peter at his sneaking, stocking, and stalking, with tiptoes light as a feather. We got many more salt blocks then we had before. And as for aiding me, she was just as helpful. Sue Ling wrote all the documents, her fingers tapping the keyboard with efficiency.

"Saving Lucky's weekly number of seals, salt blocks, and overall success has increased like wild fire. I think all this is due not only to our faithful workers from the beginning, but also to Sue Ling," I announced at one meeting. There was a huge outburst of applause from Peter and Dr. Ophellen, and me as well. Sue Ling simply blushed, shrugging her shoulders.

"We need more workers," she had said quietly. Dr. Ophellen nodded to show his agreement. He told us that he had a few partners of his that were interested in joining our cause. I put their names on a sheet of paper so I could pick them up the next day, and then turned expectantly towards Peter.

"I know this guy named Sean," he told us. "And a handful of his friends might be willing to help with Saving Lucky." I wrote his names next to the ones Dr. Ophellen had given me, and then thanked everyone at the meeting.

Now, I was on my way to gather the guys (and girls, I found out to my utter delight) who were joining us. Dr. Ophellen had offered to take everyone for a celebratory Weddell seal catch, because if we caught three more, the amount of seals that we caught would be up to a whopping three thousand, five hundred, halfway to our goal.

Ellen, or Dr. Pelliohaus, was the first stop. She was dressed up in a huge, furry outfit, smiling bright as daylight when she saw me. "Come on, we don't want to keep the doctor waiting," she exclaimed when I rapped on her wooden cabin door. "He's very excited for the big day." I grinned and led Ellen out of the house.

Next, we picked up two-in-one, Sean and Peter. They were both working at the supply building, and had just gotten permission to leave for a few hours. It was hard to tell who was more excited: Sean, bubbling over the brim with compliments, or Peter, shivering with exhilaration.

I rounded up Sue Ling after that, followed by Joe, Mia, and Eduardo, or Dr. Gonzales. Mia was, surprisingly, around my age; she was going to turn thirteen in only a few days. Joe was Peter's age, and Eduardo were grown-ups. We all walked back to where Dr. Ophellen was waiting, hopping from foot to foot. I giggled.

"Aren't you happy!" I announced, making everyone burst out laughing. Usually the doctor was seriously and reserved, but now he was clearly anticipating the upcoming task with a newfound joy.

The rather large group followed Dr. Ophellen and I to the spot where we always caught the seals, a place where Lucky had first been seen. I got out my equipment and hacked a small hole in the ground, while cheers erupted behind me. I crouched down, silently motioning for everyone to follow my lead.

A Weddell seal popped its head up from the ground three minutes after we'd settled down in our positions. With a quick swish, I wrapped it up in a net and yanked it carefully from the freezing cold water. Dr. Ophellen gave it a couple drops of medicine, then placed a salt lick in front of it. The seal sniffed the mineral block, and started to eat away at it. I smiled, but said nothing. We needed to catch more.

Sue Ling, of course, was the second one to get a seal. She was faster than wind as she gave it the medicine, let it lick the salt and nutrients, and let it go back to the ocean once it was done. Mia, Joe, Sean, and Dr. Emerson caught the next few, then Dr. Gonzales caught five in a row, a world-record for an individual, at least according to the Saving Lucky team.

"Incredible!" Dr. Ophellen yelled. "Now we're at eighty! Keep going, don't pay attention to me!" Of course, everyone ignored that, because the doctor was dancing the Turkey Trot all around the place, practically squawking in delight.

I laughed and continued to wait for the seals to pop up, Sean on one side, Mia on the other side of me. Suddenly, there came a gasp from Dr. Ophellen. Everyone looked up, of course, we weren't looking at him until then because he was so occupied dancing for joy.

"I got a page from my automatic alerting system," Dr. Ophellen cried. "Lucky's heart is completely unstable! Abbie, Sue Ling, Peter, come with me. The rest of you stay. I'm going to ask Dr. Pelliohaus to be in charge." With that, the four of us were swept away, hurrying to go check on Lucky.

My favorite Weddell seal was floating in her aquarium, not seeming to have the energy to be able to even propel herself across the water. I pressed my nose against the glass, my breath fogging my view. "What's happening?" I asked Dr. Ophellen, my own heart unstable with too much beating.

"It isn't as bad as I thought," he replied, his voice a bit calmer than before. "The abnormal pumping is almost an after shock, a left-over instability due to the upset stomach issues Lucky had before. Thank goodness it wasn't what I thought."

I nodded in relief. Lucky was lucky once more. She always was, I knew she would always be. Lucky seemed - she seemed so resilient. She was tough. She was enduring. I felt a surge of emotion rush through me, and the tears came. I sobbed in happy relief, Sue Ling and Peter joining in. They both felt the same way about Lucky, and I was so fortunate to have them.

"All right, we better stop crying, and get back to the catching," I said after a while of letting my tears of joy flow freely. Dr. Ophellen was handling Lucky on his own, so I went back to the sea-ice with Sue Ling and Peter. I watched the look on Dr. Ophellen on the way out, much happier than he had been, even back when he was dancing on the ice. He was truly happy about Lucky.

The catching was going extremely well. Fueled by the news that Lucky was healthy, the team began to sweep in even more Weddell seals, faster and faster by the second. I end up catching three in only ten minutes, which was pretty rare for me.

Our group moved down the shore about five miles before we stopped and returned to the lab for a celebration party. Dr. Ophellen had a buffet-style table laid out, with some of his famous pot roast, and hot dogs and a bunch of other food Sue Ling and Dr. Pelliohaus had cooked. I helped myself to a heaping plate filled with delicious food. I sat next to Mia at the table, and dug in.

"I'd like to make a toast," Peter announced, clanging a plastic knife to his plastic cup. "To Lucky, to Abbie, to everyone here!" Everyone shouted in agreement and took a sip of their beverages.

We chatted amongst ourselves, continuing to get many more helpings. The night wore on, and my mom came to pick me up. When she asked why we were celebrating, Dr. Ophellen quickly 'explained' that we were throwing an early goodbye party for me.

"How sweet!" she'd said. I gulped down a smile and waved to the remaining Saving Lucky members before disappearing into the snow. It was coming down harder and harder, swirling around with a fierce hostility. I remembered Tony's warning about the snowstorm. I shivered. I hoped it wouldn't get in the way of Saving Lucky.

The next morning was a quick one. I barely had time to eat my breakfast before Peter came to pick me up. Dr. Ophellen needed two people to look after the lab while he and the rest of our organization's members went out to strengthen even more seals.

Mia and I ended up staying behind. We played around with Lucky, giving her treats after she 'learned tricks'. I heated some hot chocolate on the stove, the real kind, not the tasteless, yet still fabulous, fake cocoa Dr. Ophellen always made for us. I poured the steaming liquid into two cups, gave one to Mia, and sipped the other.

"What kind of scientists are your parents?" I asked, curious. I hadn't gotten to know anything about Mia or her background since Saving Lucky rocketed into success. I knew her name was Mia, and that was about it.

"Um, I live with my aunt," Mia said quietly. She looked down at her lap, moving her lips around uncomfortably. I hoped I wasn't pressuring her. "My dad left me when my mom died in a car accident. I mean, I'm not that sad. I barely knew them." Her voice went up down an octave.

"Oh, I'm sorry," I apologized. "Maybe I shouldn't have

asked that. How about- hey, what's your favorite thing to do?" The question would probably lighten the mood. It always did for me. I could babble on and on about reading, sketching, and anything that captured my interest.

"Horses," Mia replied quickly. Her eyes were lighting up and I could tell she loved them. "They're the best animals ever. No offense to you, of course. I just think horses rock. They are so gentle, and so shy. They're - they're just like me." I smiled.

"For me, it's every animal," I told her. "I love them all." We sat there in comfortable silence, sipping our hot cocoa, thinking about everything. I was glad I hadn't joined the rest of the team at the seal-catching and strengthening place. Mia was a really nice girl. I would miss her when I left the Station.

There came a beeping from one corner of the room. I shrugged towards Mia and walked over, picking up a phone. On the screen, in clear, plain writing, was a message from Dr. Ophellen. "'Mia, stay where you are. Abbie, come join us,'" I read aloud.

"Go," Mia said. "I truly don't mind waiting here." With that consent, I ran from the lab and kept running until I reached Dr. Ophellen, crowded around by Peter, Dr. Pelliohaus, Sean, and Joe. Dr. Gonzales and Sue Ling were somewhere else; I didn't know where they had disappeared.

Dr. Ophellen looked up from the seal he was holding, his eyes squinted in disgust. When he saw me, he simply jutted his chin out, signaling for me to come over. I gasped when my eyes gazed over the brand name imprinted on the seal's skin: Amanda Tessler &

Co.

"She is so, so..." I couldn't think of an adjective that summed up Amanda all in one. "She is already in prison." I decided to use a lame threat in an attempt to make things lighter, but nothing got lighter. In fact, the snow began to come down hard just then, as if the sky shared my anger. Dr. Ophellen covered the seal in a blanket and directed everyone back toward the lab.

Mia was still there, her mug of cocoa resting in the sink. I saw she'd reheated mine, then winked at her, trying to show my thanks. "Well, I guess we're staying here for the night," I said, laughing without anything being funny. I helped Dr. Pelliohaus gently disinfect the imprint of Amanda's company on the seal, and then let the seal in with Lucky. They seemed to like each other, swimming around and sharing the food we gave them.

"I have some blankets and pillows in the back," Dr. Ophellen announced. "Sean, Joe, Peter, please go get them. Dr. Pelliohaus, Mia, and Abbie, I'd like you to help me inflate the emergency mattresses I have here." I filled each one of them with a pump and blew up seven thick beds for all of us.

Once we'd positioned everything, and the blankets were heated up, I settled into my cozy arrangement and sighed. At least my parents didn't have to worry; Dr. Pelliohaus had phoned them, using the station communication system that could call every dorm at the entire McMurdo Station, so that problem was solved. As for entertainment, it turned out that Dr. Ophellen had tons of books, and a few video games for the boys.

"Oh, I've read that!" Mia exclaimed when she saw Dr. Ophellen's copy of *Wuthering Heights*. "It's so good, isn't it?" I was delighted that Mia was another classics-girl like me. We spent half an hour discussing our favorite books, authors, and characters. Mia told me that in addition to horses, she also loved writing. That was a quality I'd never possessed, so I was immediately intrigued.

"Okay, everyone, it's now eleven o'clock," Peter reported. "Lights off, but if you'd like to stay up later, you're welcome to some flashlights." He motioned to Dr. Ophellen, who was pointing to a box in the corner. I shook my head. I was too tired.

"Goodnight," Mia whispered, her frizzy hair showing with the dim flare of a flashlight. She winked at me, our unofficial, unannounced signal.

"Goodnight," I whispered back. A second later, despite the dropping temperature, howling winds, and snoring, which I suspected to be coming from Peter, I fell asleep. The night settled over top of the McMurdo Sound, snow coming just like Tony had said. I was cozy in the lab, but still, I knew the snowstorm would delay everything. Saving Lucky was the most important thing it would postpone.

When I woke up the next morning, the sound of the cappuccino machine pounded in my ears. I blinked my stiff eyes. Where was I?! I soon remembered everything from the night before, and realized I was in Dr. Ophellen's lab, sleeping on an inflated mattress.

Sean passed around coffee and hot cocoa to everyone, then

heated up some frozen pancakes. I ate everything hungrily, since I hadn't eaten in ten hours. I'd slept in until nine o'clock in the morning, although it wasn't unusual for anyone else. We'd all woken up at about the same time.

Dr. Ophellen distributed some clothes; snow pants and flannel shirts for the boys, the same thing for the girls, only smaller. I wondered when he'd gotten all this, but didn't ask. I was just happy to have new apparel. I changed into the attire with Mia and Dr. Pelliohaus in the bathrooms, and got ready back there as well. We did the best we could with Dr. Pelliohaus's emergency kit, which included only clearance sale products.

"I don't see how we're going to get out of here," Dr. Ophellen said grimly, staring out the window. The snow was coming down so hard that I couldn't even see the buildings a hundred feet in front of the lab. I pulled out a board game and began to play, hoping the day would sort of melt away. I didn't want to concentrate on the hours, the days, the small weeks left that I was wasting in my extended month.

After two hours of Apples to Apples, I was driven out of my mind. Peter laughed from the chair he was sitting at. "Try out this mini Gameboy Dr. Ophellen has," he suggested. "You won't be bored anymore." I reluctantly took the video game from Peter's outstretched hand.

Mia and I soon learned how to play the game, and became addicted. I felt the hours slip out of my grasp, flying away like the wind. The day would be over, so would the storm. I chanted that over and over again in my head while playing on the Gameboy.

Dinner came, and the storm didn't pass. I didn't heap my plate as gleefully as I had the night before, only taking a few servings of the macaroni, and a single slice of apple pie. Dr. Ophellen noticed this, but said nothing.

"The weather reports say this storm won't stop until next week," Sean told the whole group. "I watched it on Dr. Ophellen's TV, of course. The Australian Network tells us some pretty useful stuff about Antarctica."

"That's in, like, five days," Peter groaned. "An entire school week." The rest of us grumbled as well. It was going to be a long time away from the rest of the McMurdo Station, a long time to survive on frozen food and Mrs. Smith's pies. I shoveled down the rest of my meal and went back to the Gameboy, only to find it needed to be charged, so Dr. Ophellen took all the video games and plugged them in. I pulled out my book and continued to read.

It was at about nine o'clock when we heard a single bang coming from the door. None of us paid attention, thinking it was simply the wind, persisting on making us jump. However, it came again, followed by a voice this time.

"This is the Inspectors Committee," the man boomed. "Checking to make sure everyone here is safe." Dr. Ophellen motioned quietly for us to cover Lucky's aquarium, and for me, Mia, Joe, Sean, and Peter to all pretend to be asleep. Dr. Pelliohaus took her position, reading in one corner.

"Yes?" he called out into the cold, opening the door. The

man stepped in, smiling. He counted everyone, thanked Dr. Ophellen, and handed him a package. "What's that?" Dr. Ophellen asked.

"Some more frozen food," the inspector told him. "It's all we can get. Oh, and there's some entertainment in there as well, and some extra blankets. We're sorry that this storm is an inconvenience, sir. The only reason we could get out here is because we have our handy Inspectors truck!" And with that, the inspector left.

Everyone resumed to their normal activities, but this time, Mia and I could read some gossip magazines the 'Inspectors Committee' had by miracle delivered, the boys could play new video games, and Dr. Pelliohaus and Dr. Ophellen could read some interesting new books about science. We almost seemed like a family, cozying up on a snowy day.

"We should be getting to bed soon," I whispered to Mia. Already I felt the need to rest; in the morning Mia and I had a secret plan to try to sneak out of the lab and see if we could survive the storm. "We need the rest."

Mia nodded, and together we changed into our pajamas. I snuggled under my covers, smiling to myself. Before two seconds passed, or before you could say, "Saving Lucky!" I was sound, sound asleep.

Dreams of snowflakes and hot chocolate and seals danced through my head. I kept seeing a face, a cute little Weddell seal face. Lucky was always smiling, in some way; I didn't know how she could be so cute. I dreamt I was swimming in the ocean with her, and other sea creatures joined us, like the whales and seals and fish. We were all peaceful, all getting along. I swam as if I were a mermaid flapping my feet gently but getting propelled at surprising speed.

"Wake up!" a fish whispered. I turned my head, confused, towards the little guppy. My eyes widened. It wasn't a guppy - it was Mia! I realized I had been asleep, dreaming, and Mia had just told me to wake up. I stretched, yawning... something was important that day... I couldn't figure out what.

"Oh, my gosh," I yelped, sitting up in bed. "Surviving the storm!" Mia gave me the stink eye and put a finger to her already lip-glossed lips. I ran to the bathroom, trying to get ready as fast as I could, as fast as I could have in my dream.

We snuck out the back door, and were greeted by the freezing, harsh winds. The snow whipped around us howling like a lone wolf. I shivered even though I was packed into six, thick, fuzzy layers. Mia rubbed her gloves together in an attempt to keep her hands warm.

"I-I don't know about this," I shouted above the ruckus. Where was Mia? I couldn't see her anywhere, with the flurries of snow swirling around me like cyclones. "Mia! Mia!" I shouted her name, trying to call out even with the shrieking wind.

I stepped through the snow, calling out 'Mia!' wherever I went. Suddenly, I heard a whimper beneath me. I took my toe off the unusually hard patch of ground, and knelt down to see Mia lying there. Her teeth were chattering; she could barely move.

"Hypothermia," I mumbled in fear. "Oh no. Mia? Mia, can you hear me?" When she half-nodded, I was relieved the cold hadn't taken over completely. I tried to lift her up, which automatically failed, since Mia was limp. I finally ended up dragging and pulling her across the snow, and back to the lab, where everyone was sure to be anxiously awaiting our arrival.

Indeed, once I pulled Mia inside the building with an exhausted sigh, Dr. Pelliohaus wrapped her up in a blanket, told Sean to get some medicine out from the storage area, and then snuggled me in a blanket, too. I took a sip of the steaming hot chocolate she'd made before explaining the short, but terrifying, story.

Mia came back to the main room, her face looking healthier (and prettier) than the ugly white color it had been when she was stuck in the snow. "Thank you so much, Sean." She thanked him then turned to me. "And Abbie, as well. We never should have tried to sneak out!" Everyone moaned, and shook their heads in agreement. We sat around for a while, and watched Mia turn normal and chatty again.

"Hello, everyone," Dr. Ophellen said sleepily, hobbling into the room, still wearing his fuzzy robe. "I might have a few movies in the back, does anyone -"

"I'm already there!" Joe crowed, making everyone chuckle again. We all raced to where the doctor kept his TV, and waited for him to show the collection. It was surprisingly big; I decided he collected them as a secret hobby. I voted for a holiday movie, an old favorite; *A Christmas Story*, the one where the boy wants a BB gun, but everyone says, "You'll shoot your eye out!"

The one I chose ended up winning, so we all laughed at the little boy's antics, and voted for Favorite Moment, Funniest Scene, Weirdest Person, Wackiest Plan, and so on. We had a great time, watching classics and being funny and pigging out. Everything was calm again, the hypothermia episode almost forgotten.

Those next few days passed the same, playing games, reading, drawing, and having fun. I learned how to dissect an old, dead frog from Dr. Ophellen, mastered the skill of mouth-whistling from Joe, and committed to memory a lot of other cool tricks I learned from my stuck-in-a-lab mates.

My mom and dad were kept up to date every day along with the other people in the dorms of McMurdo Station, thanks to Dr. Pelliohaus. She was a very nice lady, and I became a good friend of hers. She was fantastic at telling stories, stories that made you squeal and laugh and feel a tingle go down your spine.

On Sunday, a week later, once I'd just opened my sticky, sleepy eyes, a ray of sunlight peeked into the lab. I jumped up, shouting in joy, "THE SUN! THE SUN!" Everyone got up, tired as I had been, and immediately began to rejoice. We ate a last breakfast and hugged everyone goodbye, and then parted ways to go see our families, or go back to our dorms and relax. I couldn't wait to see my parents, even if the stay at the lab had been fun.

When I reached Building 9, they were waiting outside waving big signs that told me I was definitely welcomed back. I laughed and ran to them, letting myself be scooped up in a ginormous bear hug, like I was a little kid. I didn't care if they treated me as if I was young, I was just glad to be back.

"Oh, we missed you, darling," my mom said sentimentally, a tear forming in her eye. I smiled, and let her be sappy. I kissed her on the cheek, then moved onto Dad, who lifted me into the air, something he'd stopped doing when I was three. I felt happy, soaring above the 'clouds', flying in my dad's arms.

"I missed you too," I whispered.

Back in the dorm, I changed into some fresh clothes of mine, some cozy sweatpants and a Harvard sweatshirt. My dad turned on the TV and fell asleep in a few minutes, my mom joining him. I was exhausted as well, but I couldn't sleep. When my parents finally woke up, I pretended I had slept as well, and woken up right before them.

"Does this shorten my time here?" I wondered aloud to Mom. She pursed her lips, and looked over at my dad. *Sweetheart, of course. Nature takes its own path, just like that father of yours always says,* I knew she was going to say, I just knew it.

"Yes, dear," she answered. "You have about another week before we have to pack up." I nodded a reluctant acceptance, after all, I had to face it: I couldn't stay here forever, even though I desperately wanted to. I'd come to realize that.

With a quick kiss from my mom, and a hug from my dad, I was off again, to help with Saving Lucky. I hoped Sue Ling and Dr. Gonzalez would be there, since they hadn't come with Dr.

94

Ophellen's crew on the day after our celebratory catching event.

"Thank goodness you're here, Abbie," Dr. Ophellen exclaimed when I arrived at the lab. "Hardly anyone can help today at the lab. Sean is on make-up work time at the supply building, and he also offered to cover Peter's time as well; Peter is out catching and strengthening with Sue Ling; Dr, Gonzalez is getting some salt blocks from anther research center; Mia is with her aunt; Dr. Pelliohaus is going on an expedition and she won't be coming back until three weeks from now; and Joe's parents are leaving tomorrow!" My eyes widened when I heard how fast he was talking, and also at the terrible news of Joe's departure. He was a good helper.

I offered to stay at the lab, watch Lucky, clean, and do everything Dr. Ophellen needed to do. I swept the entire place first, then scrubbed every single thing there until it gleamed. I organized the TV, movie collection, games, and magazines, and finally, prepared a lunch for the helpers and some hot apple cider and tea for everyone. I wasn't that good with the coffee machine yet, and I didn't want to mess it up.

"Wow, Abbie, this is great!" Peter said as he trampled in through the door. He helped himself to the lunch, and ate hardily. Dr. Ophellen and Sue Ling got the same amount of food as Peter, but they drank the tea instead of cider.

"I have an announcement to make," the doctor declared once everyone had finished eating their desserts. "From the past few weeks, and with the help of all our incredible Saving Lucky members, we've caught exactly four thousand, nine hundred ninety nine seals. I saved the last Weddell seal for the founder of this organization: Abbie." And then there was applause, big applause, and I got to go to the area where I'd first seen Lucky. Joe, Sean, Dr. Pelliohaus, Dr. Gonzalez and Mia were all waiting for me there, too. I suspected Joe wasn't leaving, and there really wasn't any three-week long expedition, and Dr. Gonzalez hadn't gone for salt blocks.

I leaned over a breathing hole, waiting for a perfect little seal to pop up. I waited for about three minutes before a cute pup just went, well, pop, through the hole. I smiled a millisecond before gently scooping it up in my net. After I'd carefully given it the medicine and salt lick, I cocked my head to one side.

"You are officially Lucky, Jr.!" I whispered happily, and released it back into the ocean. Cheers rang out through the air... Saving Lucky was complete. It was absolutely, wonderfully, terrifically complete. Not even Amanda could stop me now... then my mind wandered over to Lucky. Would I really have to let her go? Would I really have to?

Those thoughts were soon flying away from my head, as I went back to the cabin to rest for a while, and then went out to dinner with my parents. The day wore on with me never thinking one thing about Lucky, and the burden of having to let her go.

However, once I was snuggled down in my cot and the warm blankets piled heavily on top of my stomach, I began to see the moment which hadn't happened yet, although it had to happen sometime, where I released Lucky into the ocean and she was gone from me forever.

Gone from me forever. Could I truly survive that way, eternally separated from Lucky?

Those thoughts disturbed me greatly. I shuddered, even though I was wrapped up in cozy blankets. Saving Lucky was truly complete, but did I want it to be? I felt myself being torn in all different directions.

"Abbie? Darling, it's ten thirty," someone said. "Time to get going." I sighed and stretched. *Please, Dr. Pelliohaus, don't do this again*, I thought, then suddenly realized I was back in the dorm, not at the lab, stuck with all the Saving Lucky members, having to eat heat-up food for every meal. I gasped in relief as I hopped out of bed.

I walked with my parents to get breakfast. Peter, Sean, Joe, Sue Ling, Mia, Dr. Ophellen, Dr. Gonzalez and Dr. Pelliohaus all waved to me from their table, which they'd 'reserved' for members only. I told my mom and dad that I had to go join them, and quickly ran over to where everyone was waiting for me.

"Abbie!" Peter cried, and reached up to hug me. I hugged him back tightly, then squeezed everyone in turn. It was truly official, official that Saving Lucky had finally come to a close, official that everything, almost everything, was right. There was still Amanda, but I'd come to realize it was her loss that she was so cruel, evil, and mean. It definitely was her loss, not mine. She was on the dark side, not me. She had to deal with being hated, not me.

I had a delicious cheese omelet, toast, tea, potatoes, and fruit

97

for breakfast. Everyone filled their plates high with the delectable food, another celebration of success. I ate with the Saving Lucky members for a while, and then went back over to join my parents.

"So, I guess we're leaving soon," I said, half-smiling. I knew it would eventually be time to leave all places, no matter how long I stayed there or how much I got attached to them. Antarctica, the McMurdo Station, and everything here had been an incredible experience. I guessed I had really enjoyed my stay at the station, but knew it was time to go.

My mom nodded, grinning out of the corner of her mouth. "Yes, we'll have to pack our bags in a few days," she replied. "You had a great time here, didn't you, Abbie?" I nodded. After all, it was the complete truth.

The next couple of twenty-four hours flew by, even faster than when I'd been staying at Dr. Ophellen's lab. I read *Wuthering Heights*, and finished it at exactly seven forty six p.m., on a Tuesday. I was very proud of the fact I'd completed the book in only a month, when it took a regular book club two months to finish it. I also helped out at the lab, cleaning up after the mess the doctor made, and taking care of Lucky. I counted our precious seconds together, making sure I spent as much time as I could with her.

Those days seemed normal, calm, regular. I wanted to turn back the clock, go back to when I'd first been bouncing along in the truck, staring at the snowflakes that slid down the window, reminding me of how my life was so hectic, so deranged.

Sadly, I couldn't. I dreaded the moment when my mom came

into the room, her cheeks red from the snow and cold winds outside. "Honey, you'd better start picking up your stuff," she said. "We're leaving exactly three days from now, just to let you know." And then Dad came in, and began listing all the places he planned to go. I tuned out, and sighed.

The next day, I went down to the lab, since Dr. Ophellen had asked me to come visit him. I expected to see the whole crew there, waiting to wish me goodbye, but was surprised when it was just the doctor.

"Thank you for coming, Abbie," Dr. Ophellen said, his mouth a tight line of sorrow. I could see he was very close to tears now, sad I was going to leave. We'd become very good friends. I would also be dismal without his companionship, once I was off and away from my 'family' here.

We sat down at a table that was arranged next to Lucky's aquarium. I cleared my throat, hoping the doctor would begin to tell me when he was going to release Lucky. Of course, he remained silent, so I had to prod him. "Dr. Ophellen," I announced. "I know this is a question we've both been avoiding, but... when is Lucky leaving?"

He sat in silence for a while, staring at the floor and occasionally blinking. "Well, Abbie," he replied finally. "I was thinking today. Now, of course, since I know you and I have grown very fond of her, maybe Lucky can have a tracking device put on her, not like a GPS or anything, but something to let us know where she is, and check on her if she's in the area."

I squealed in delight. What a great idea! "Perfect!" I exclaimed. "Why didn't I think of that?" Dr. Ophellen pulled out a small needle and kit, and showed me how to gently put it on Lucky. Once my favorite Weddell seal was out of her aquarium, lying safely on the table, of course, I began to put the strap around her arm, and ease the locater close to her skin. Dr. Ophellen nodded his approval.

Lucky was gently put into a mesh crate, and the doctor drove us down to where she'd first been captured. I felt something well up in inside of me: my stomach settled to a determined stone. I knew I had to do this. Lucky couldn't stay with me forever.

I took a look around, trying to find the perfect air hole to release her into. I found one not too far down on the sea-ice, since I didn't want any injuries. I directed Dr. Ophellen to carry Lucky's cage to where I was standing.

"Would you do the honors?" Dr. Ophellen barely whispered.

I nodded and slowly unzipped the cage. I watched Lucky come out, and crawl onto the ice. I saw she wasn't exactly a pup anymore, she had grown-up. Her fluffy, playful coat had been exchanged for a serious, beautiful one, her eyes had a more practical look then a gleaming one in them; she had changed. Lucky looked up at me, and I saw an expression I would never forget.

Lucky nuzzled my leg with her nose, as if trying to say something. She made a little yipping noise, a cute whimper that melted my heart. I reached down to pet her, and Lucky didn't resist. She let me finger her soft fuzz with such delicacy that I barely felt her.

"Alright, come on, back to the ocean," I murmured, steering Lucky gently to the breathing hole. I could feel her excitement tingling through her backbone. At first I felt resentment, seeing her so cheerful, but then I realized it was for the best. She was happy, and healthy, after all, wasn't that what I'd always wanted?

Then, I saw her white tail disappear into the water, and she was gone. Lucky was truly, completely gone. I felt like putting my arm around the doctor and crying, crying until my heart fell out. However, something held me back from doing so. I simply smiled.

"She'll always be with us," I said aloud, turning back to Dr. Ophellen. "Come on, let's get back to the lab." We walked slowly back through the snow, trudging along slowly. As we did, everything I'd done here came to me at once. I imagined it was like the moment before you die, when your entire life is spread out before you.

First, I saw myself in the truck; after that, in Ivan, sighing and wishing I were still in Russia, but at the same time, happy to be somewhere else. Russia had been getting boring for me. Then it was Lucky, gorgeous and playful. She was still only a pup then, her coat slicked down from the water. I remembered petting her and how the feeling shocked me, my mom laughing, explaining why she had fur and extra blubber and all the scientific side of her cuteness. I saw Dr. Coulan defying me, then apologizing. I saw Peter, Dr. Ophellen, and Amanda, the bonfires, meeting Sue Ling; truly, truly everything, all of it had been absolutely amazing.

It made me realize that I'd always be welcomed back, always cherished at the McMurdo Station. I grinned and whistled a tune,

101

trying to cheer up the doctor. The effort was a failure; Dr. Ophellen wasn't happy at all, but I was. Lucky truly had deserved to stay with us for a while, although at some point she'd have to leave. And she just had.

"I suppose you are correct, Abbie," Dr. Ophellen admitted, when I told him my thoughts about Lucky having to go. "Everything takes its leave, at one part of life or another." I nodded. It was entirely true. Lucky and I were both going, though maybe we weren't exactly going the same way, we were leaving, both of us.

Dr. Ophellen and I stayed at the lab for a while, occasionally gazing over at the empty aquarium that used to hold Lucky. We missed her a lot. It was like she was the gravity in our worlds, and the gravity was gone. We were just floating around, trying to grab onto random things so we would stay put.

I left after awhile, my parents were waiting for me back at the dorms. They were already packing by the time I entered the room, the place smelling like old clothing. I began to gather my clothes up, folding them and putting them in my suitcase robotically. Once I was done with the apparel, I stuffed away everything I'd received since I was at the station: a stone, a few penguin feathers, and some books Dr. Pelliohaus had given me. It was all so sad, leaving a place that had become my home.

"Abbie, darling, Dr. Rose is having a chess game at her dorm," my dad announced when he saw I was done packing. "Would you like to join us?" I shook my head. I wanted to stay in bed for a while since I wasn't feeling too good.

102

My parents left, telling me to get better, since we were leaving the next day, and I stared after them, looking at the space they'd just been. I squeezed my eyes shut to re-adjust my blurred vision. With a reluctant sigh, I pulled out the latest classic book I was going to read: *Pride and Prejudice*. It was a novel my mom had always enjoyed, because she had fallen in love with it in college. She wanted me to read it very badly, so I did.

It was a good story, an enjoyable, pleasant book; I read it for hours. I got to the two hundred and tenth page before my mom burst through the door again, followed by my father. They were grinning, in the eyes and on the mouth. I could tell one of them had won... who? Neither of them was even very good at chess.

"Oh, we had a fantastic time, dear," my dad said, breathless. "I moved the queen, and bam, I won! Then, the next round, your mother did the same stellar move. It was absolutely incredible, you know. Dr. Smith, that wonderful expedition leader, he was there, and then, well, Amanda Tessler, she was there, I don't call her a doctor 'cuz she doesn't deserve the title, and also Dr. Pelliohaus, she said she knows you, and even that Dr. Ophellen, he said to say hi, and-"

I laughed. "Slow down there, Dad," I chuckled. "You can tell me all about it on the trip to, um, wherever we're going to go." After another long and excited explanation, I learned the Foresters were going to travel to the Galapagos Islands. That would be fun, I'd always wanted to go there and maybe meet a turtle. I could finally order the summer clothes from the catalog, as well.

The night passed quickly; I fell asleep easily, exhausted from the traumatizing day. I dreamt of nothing, really, just a blank white space that seemed to be cozy and warm and filled with happiness. I felt good, I had to feel good in this kind of environment, but I was still a bit uneasy. Something wasn't right about this place - I had to be peaceful, not overwhelmed like this.

I finally found my good corner of the empty space, curled up, and went into a real sleep. I woke up the next morning refreshed, ready to go. I dressed in some shorts and a cute t-shirt, then popped on some puffy pants and a fuzzy, thick parka. My boots covered bare feet, I was holding a handbag that contained flip-flops. I was fully prepared for the Galapagos.

On the way to the airway, I picked up Peter and Dr. Ophellen. "You'll take care of Amanda, right?" I asked them, more of stating something than asking a question. When they nodded, I giggled. Of course the doctor and Peter would.

Right before I was about to get on the aircraft, the small, bumbling thing I feared could break any second; Peter stepped up to me, holding out a little red box. My name, my full name, spelled out in fancy, gold, velvet letters, was on the top. I carefully opened the silver latch and gasped.

"Oh, it's beautiful!" I exclaimed, fingering the necklace in my hand. Indeed, it was beautiful. The charm on it was in the shape of a Weddell seal, the eyes little diamonds, gleaming just like Lucky's. On it, letters even smaller than the ones on the box spelled out McMurdo Station Memories. I smiled. "Thank you so much, Peter." We hugged each other in front of the adults, which was a little awkward, but I enjoyed the moment. Peter would always be my friend.

I exchanged goodbyes with Dr. Ophellen in turn then went up the white staircase coming from the bottom of the airplane. I stopped at the top, looking out over the McMurdo Sound. It was a big mass of snow, rocks, buildings, and the people I knew and loved. I smiled, savoring the view.

The same feeling I'd had when I was releasing Lucky flooded over me, spilling onto the snowflake-filled ground below. I gave a final wave to Peter and Dr. Ophellen below, shouted goodbye, and turned my back on them. I stepped into the airplane with a new confidence, a new feeling.

Saving Lucky. I'd truly finished!

Epilogue

Abigail Forester, now twenty-three years old, stepped out of Ivan and thanked the driver, doing her classic tip-him-and-he-serves-you-forever trick. She waited patiently on the snow-covered ground for her new husband, Peter, to emerge. He was so tall that his lean frame barely fit through the door.

"Was the ride bumpy?" Abigail laughed, when she saw Peter's practically green face. Her spouse simply nodded, and clutched his stomach. He held Abigail's hand with his gloved one, and together they raced to the memorable slope where Lucky had first been discovered.

There was a small breathing hole there, just a small tiny one. Peter pointed it out to Abigail. "Look, darling," he exclaimed. "There's a seal popping out!" Sure enough, there was one, surfacing to gasp up some air. Abigail squinted hard, trying to make out the strangely familiar green band on its fin.

"Do you - give me some binoculars," Abigail demanded to Peter, her hand outstretched. Peter obeyed, and reached into his backpack to supply his wife with her need. Abigail put the binoculars to her eyes, staring directly at the seal.

For one, she knew that the seal was a female Weddell, and second, she knew it was Lucky. Abigail squealed in delight. "It's Lucky!" she shouted, dancing on the spot. She ran down the slope, not caring if her carefully groomed ponytail was flying out in an amber flame behind her. Abigail flung herself close to the hole hoping and praying her Weddell seal would recognize her.

Lucky saw the human girl in front of her. She knew her from somewhere, a while back, a long time ago. Lucky had a flashback of times before, the human girl caring for her, the kind doctor-man feeding her medicine, the girl gently releasing her back into the sea. It was her! The one the humans called Abbie! Lucky reached her fins onto the ice and flopped next to the girl, nuzzling her arm.

Abigail couldn't believe it. So she did! Lucky did recognize her! She reached down and patted the seal, feeling Lucky's fur once again. She was submerged in memories; caring for Lucky, Dr. Ophellen giving her medicine and the mineral blocks, releasing Lucky back into the ocean.

"Peter!" she called. "It's her, it's really her!" Abigail's spouse followed his wife's footsteps, slipped in them, and slid all the way to where Abigail waited, laughing silently, her shaking shoulders giving away her laughter. Peter rolled his eyes, ignoring her, and reached down to pet Lucky. She felt so funny, so cute, just like a pup.

"You're right," Peter whispered.

There was a male too, the one 'Abbie' had been friends with when she was still a little girl human. He had been an acquaintance then,

107

but now he was something more. Lucky could sense he had grown attached to Abbie, and also to something - something that pointed to herself, Lucky. Perhaps he was just as fond of her as Abbie had been, and clearly still was.

The threesome stayed there on the ice, Abigail with her arm around Peter's waist, her free hand stroking Lucky's soft skin, Peter embracing Abigail back, yet still showing his affection for Lucky.

Abigail and Peter went to their new dorm later after spending plenty of time with Lucky. On the way back, they contemplated their favorite moments spent with Lucky, and many other moments they had shared at McMurdo Station.

"Remember when you gave me that beautiful necklace?" Abigail giggled. "I loved it so much, I wore it until my mom threatened to cut it off me because I'd never take it off." Peter's eyes floated into the past, remembering that moment.

"Do you still have it?" he asked. Abigail was surprised; she'd thought he would, for certain, make fun of how strange he was back then. Instead, he asked if she still kept the necklace. Abigail nodded without hesitation, reached into her purse, and pulled out the tiny Weddell seal charm and chain.

"How sweet," Peter whispered. He pulled in Abigail for a kiss, thinking only of the time when he'd given her the necklace. Peter knew he'd always love Abigail, love her for being a kind, beautiful woman, love her for being a sweet friend, love her for loving Lucky.

Lucky could sense something was going on between the male and Abbie now, something she'd always wanted to see. With all her effort, Lucky pushed her way up the slope, and stared out at the tall structures the humans had built. She felt a warm tingle go up her spine when she saw Abbie embracing the male. She'd always known they'd make a good pair. They were the ones who made saving her possible, after all.

They made Saving Lucky possible.

Author's Note

The McMurdo Station, Weddell Seals, and All Characters in *Saving Lucky*

All characters, human and animal alike, are completely fictitious, but the setting, however, isn't. The McMurdo Station is a real research station on Ross Island, Antarctica. I, the author, Isabella Alvarez, did a lot of research in order to find out more about the station, and the animals there as well. Here are some key facts about the McMurdo Station in general.

○ The McMurdo Station is owned by the NSF, the National Science Foundation.

○ The McMurdo Station was named after Lieutenant Archibald McMurdo, of the H.M.S. *Terror.*

○ The McMurdo Station has signed the Antarctic Treaty, which 'regulates intergovernmental relations with respect to Antarctica.'

○ The average temperature of December, which is the time of the year *Saving Lucky* occurs, is -0.8 degrees Celsius.

○ McMurdo Station has both Internet and voice communications (Skype).

- When Abbie is leaving the Station, she travels by the Sea Ice Runway, which is an annual runway built on the sea-ice near the McMurdo Station, but there are two other 'airports' - the Pegasus Ice Runway, and William's Field.
- The Station has been mentioned in many films, books, and poems, such as in Kim Stanley Robinson's science fiction novel *Antarctica;* in Sarah Andrews' *In Cold Pursuit*, is based in the Station; in Werner Herzog's documentary, *Encounters at the End of the World*, which deals with individuals living at the McMurdo Station; and finally, McMurdo Station is referred to in the science fiction movies *Dark Star* and *Alien* as being a site of a major space-traffic control center

Weddell seals also make a big appearance through this book. They are absolutely incredible creatures, distinctive members of the pinniped family. The facts below are about Weddell seals.
- Weddell seals are least concerned on the conservation status.
- Male Weddell seals, unlike most seal breeds, weigh less than the female seals. They weigh about 1,110 pounds, while the females can be slightly larger or heavier.
- Weddell seals gather in small groups or are sometimes solitary.

○ The Weddell seal's metabolism is constant during deep-water dives, in which they can stay under water for approximately 80 minutes. They come up for breath regularly, though, and thus they 'pop' up from under the sea ice.

On Abbie's tour with the great (and loud) Dr. Smith, she rides Junior to see some incredible birds that don't fly: Emperor Penguins. I've always had a fascination with these adorable, hardy creatures, so I decided to put them in the story, since they're a big part of Antarctica, and also of the McMurdo Station. Here are some facts about Emperor Penguins.

○ Emperor Penguins are the tallest and heaviest penguins in all of Antarctica.

○ They are most known for the journey the female adults take every year, in which they forage at the sea and carry back plenty of fish.

○ The Emperor Penguin's typical lifespan is about 20 years, but some scientific observations suggest that some of these incredible birds might live to 50 years old.

○ An Emperor Penguin can hold their breath for 20 minutes, and can dive to depths over 1,800 feet.

For more information check out some of the websites below:

www.nsf.org The National Science Foundation website is a reliable place where you can learn about McMurdo Station, scientific research, why they're protecting Antarctica, and so on.

www.nationalgeographic.com Look up information on many animals and places around the globe, including Antarctica and McMurdo Station. I recommend the kids part to watch informative, funny videos.

www.youtube.com Search 'dorms at McMurdo' and you can view a video of someone touring the dorms and walking around on the crunchy surface snow, which is a mixture of volcanic rocks and snow.

Finally, I'd just like to say that the McMurdo Station, Antarctica, and all its inhabitants are absolutely incredible. As they say, Antarctica is the Switzerland of science!

Acknowledgements

First, I'd like to thank my mom, dad, and wonderful writing teacher, Miss Lili. They have always encouraged me to shoot for the stars, to reach for the moon if I fall, and to always keep writing!

Then, I'm incredibly grateful to NaNoWriMo, for encouraging me to follow my dream. Thank you for supporting me in a new way, since NaNoWriMo was new to me.

Of course, I owe a big time thanks to my writing inspirations -- J.K. Rowling, C.S. Lewis, Erin Hunter, and many other authors, the ones who make me push myself to write everyday. You guys are absolutely incredible. I want to be just like you when I grow up, a fantastic author and an interesting person.

My friends, especially the ones who're joining me on my quest to conquer NaNoWriMo -- Olivia T., and Sofia P., you are both great writers and am sure you'll go far with your writing. Also, to my amazing friends who simply cheer me on from the sidelines, thank you.

Then, there's the ol' teacher gratitude expression, for me, it's not a same old, same old thing -- my teachers are truly fantastic! Mr. Aiello, you inspire me to write a lot of quirky things. Mrs. Cohen, you are a very awesome math and science teacher, and I'm praying for you to get better.

And finally, I'm grateful for this book. I'm thanking myself, for writing it; Abbie, for being an incredible main character, your guts and courage and determination inspire me to be just like you; Peter, for being a good helper to my awesome Abbie, you are funny and still a human boy, who can have his annoying doubts; Dr. Ophellen, for having the knowledge and experience of being a highly scientific person, you make me take on a whole new side of writing, about an adult who is actually trustworthy, and not even making a single mistake; Amanda, for having the quality of an interesting antagonist, you are a wonderful actress... or are you truly sinister?! And also to the rest of the fantastic characters and settings, all of the things in this book, they're all incredible. Hands down incredible.

Made in the USA
Lexington, KY
21 March 2012